(songs for lovers)
give me

irina denezhkina
translated from the russian
by andrew bromfield

SIMON & SCHUSTER
NEW YORK   LONDON   TORONTO   SYDNEY

Simon & Schuster
Rockefeller Center
1230 Avenue of the Americas
New York, NY 10020

Originally published in Russian in 2002 by Limbus Press

SIMON & SCHUSTER and colophon are registered trademarks
of Simon & Schuster, Inc.
For information about special discounts for bulk purchases,
please contact Simon & Schuster Special Sales at
1-800-456-6798 or business@simonandschuster.com

Designed by Davina Mock

Manufactured in the United States of America

10 9 8 7 6 5 4 3 2 1

Library of Congress Cataloging-in-Publication Data

Denezhkina, Irina.
[Dai mne! English]
Give me: songs for lovers/Irina Denezhkina; translated from the Russian by
    Andrew Bromfield
    p. cm.
Contents: Give me!—Valerochka—Song for lovers—Vasya and the green
men—Remote feelings—Lyokha the rottweiler—My beautiful Ann—
Postscript—Death in the chat room—You and me—Isupov. 1. Denezhkina,
Irina—Translations into English. I. Bromfield, Andrew. II. Title.
PG3491.6.E64D4613 2005
891.7'35—dc22   2004058902
ISBN 978-0-7432-5464-9

To Nigger, LenuSik, Nasska and Casper

contents

give me!

You froze, my joy, eyes startled wide,
The snow swept over you and me.
The drifts lay deep on every side,
We sought each other, but couldn't see.
                                    BANDerlogi

What d'you want? Coffee?"

Lyapa stood in the middle of the room, naked from the waist up, confused and sweaty. His underwear was sticking out of the top of his pants. I felt like saying "You," but I thought that would only lead to even greater confusion and he might simply take root where he stood. Just stand there like a statue. Then what would I do?

"Coffee? Or tea?"

"Coffee, coffee . . ."

Relieved, Lyapa reached into a cupboard, switched on the kettle, rummaged in the fridge and took out some milk. Dived back into the fridge and took out a bottle of beer. Then another. Opened one and began sucking on it greedily.

1

I sat down at the table, propping my head up on my hands. Lyapa's hair sticks up, twisted into spikes like a hedgehog's. He has two silver rings in his ear, a big nose and big round eyes like a puppy. He's like a puppy all over: fidgety, bouncy, soft and bendy. As my girlfriend Volkova says—"makes you want to squeeze and hug him." Lyapa's beautiful. His dream is he's walking down the street and girls run up to him yelling "Lyapa! Lyapa!" desperate to give him a blowjob. Lyapa plays punk rock and wants to be famous. And he wants me to stop sitting here like a fool and embarrassing him. Or maybe he doesn't. I can't see that deep into the darkness of his soul.

The kettle boiled. Lyapa spooned out some coffee for me, then sugar, poured over the boiling water. He sat down facing me and began smoking intently. Staring fixedly at the bridge of my nose. A word about me: I'm three inches taller than Lyapa, with long dark hair, brown eyes, an immensely high opinion of myself and the figure of a model. That's what one guy told me, but I know it wouldn't hurt to slim a bit and my stomach's not flat from working out, it's because I don't eat much.

Anyway, Lyapa's my husband. We got married online, or actually he married me; all I did was passively click "Yes." The jerk had seen my photos, but he didn't send his own. Wrote that he didn't have one, said he didn't have a scanner or some other excuse. Volkova and I conferred about it and decided he was probably an ugly freak. Fuck him, we decided. Volkova sighed dramatically and made an elegant gesture with her hand. Then he suggested meeting in the metro. We didn't have anything else to do, so we went to meet him, but prepared ourselves for disappointment in advance.

We're standing there drop-dead gorgeous in the metro. I've got on this skintight T-shirt and shorts that end before they've hardly begun. Volkova's in a long sky-blue dress that shows everybody her boobs and her backside, everything big and bouncy. Her light brown hair's all carefully styled and lacquered—"Not like you: Rake it across the bald patch and off you go." A big nose. It doesn't spoil her though. It gives her individuality. All the men stare hard when she walks past. And when we're together, it's like the end of the world.

There we are standing opposite the escalator, with people riding up and out in our direction. All sorts.

"Look at that one; what an ugly kisser!"

"He's looking in our direction! Yuh-uck!"

"Anyone but that one, anyone but that one!"

"Oh, sugar . . . no, don't come this way!"

"No, not that freak, please!"

So we're standing there whispering, and in the end we wound ourselves up so much we almost legged it top-speed out of the metro. But for some reason we hung on. Then suddenly I see two boys coming toward us. The one who's not so tasty is like a Soviet soft toy dog. The other's Pepsi, pager, MTV, spiky hair, fruit-drop lips, really cocky look. Gorgeous like a picture in a magazine.

"Which of you is my husband?" I asked in a voice hoarse with excitement, while Volkova digested the information. "No need to run; the beauty contest's come to you."

"Me," the gorgeous one answered modestly. "I'm Lyapa. And this is Kres."

Kres shook his long hair and smiled in a village-yokelish kind of way. Round-faced and round-bellied. Lyapa beamed.

And now here I am sitting in his kitchen, and he's smoking and not showing the slightest sign of interest. He's two years younger than me.

I downed my coffee decisively, burnt my tongue, got up and made for the door.

"Where are you going?" Lyapa said, rousing himself.

"Home!"

"It's nighttime. You can't go out there."

"So what do I do?"

Lyapa started thinking. Maybe he'd overdone it back then on the Net, when he showered me with messages: "My pussycat! I love you very, very much!" Maybe he shouldn't have. It's two months now since that meeting in the metro. We see each other once a week. I've been with Volkova to watch his band rehearse a couple of times. I remember the guitarist Vitya sang a line instead of Kres, and Kres was really upset and took offense, because he's the vocalist, not Vitya. He was humiliated in front of Volkova and me. He was left with nothing to do. As if he weren't the vocalist at all, just some piece of gear that could easily be replaced. Take Lyapa: I don't think you could replace him; no one else plays the drums like that. But Kres . . . Like, who cares?

Volkova had them figured out right away: nice boys, not bad-looking boys, like a set of matching dolls, but they were "nothing but a bunch of teenagers." Volkova plays her own field: rich men. Lyapa & Co. were left to me. But all they were for me was "nothing but" too. I don't know why. Some "husband" I have!

"Shall I see you home?"

I decided to strike a pose and declared:

"I can get there on my own. I'm not a child!"

Lyapa and I live at opposite ends of town. I only have to go around the corner from Lyapa's place to the metro, but then I have to ride for almost an hour all the way over to the Vyborg District. "Okay, but when you get there give me a call."

I didn't answer and slammed the door. Some husband . . . Hah! Just a messy situation.

Some young guy smashed out of his skull trailed after me from the bus stop—really tall, long hair and black glasses, clutching a bottle of Petrovskoe beer. I kept walking and kept my mouth shut, cursing Lyapa and cursing myself for wanting God knows what. Who's he to me anyway?

Meanwhile this lowlife has started grabbing at my arm and hassling me, raising his voice. I got frightened. He was drunk, after all.

"Wassya name, sweetart? Why don'choo tell me? G'won, tell me! I'm Vova!"

A crowd of teenage kids appeared, coming toward us. Great, I thought. That's all I need. Then I'll send Lyapa to hell for sure, with a big bunch of roses.

The crowd came closer. Out in front of them this dirty little kid of about twelve was dancing around. He was the one who said it.

"It's him, guys!"

They separated Vova from me with a neat smack to his mouth. The bottle of beer swung loose out of Vova's hands and went flying into the air. I stood there and watched, stupefied, as several guys jumped up and down on Vova's head while the others put the boot into his gut. I wanted to do something, but it was like my arms and legs had gone numb. I only vaguely remember what happened next. There were about twenty guys giving Vova a vicious kicking. He was groaning and howling. He tried to fend them off with his arms, rolling from side to side, always coming up against their Doc Martens. The blood spread across the pavement in a dark puddle.

People gathered around, curious. Two fat men, a granny with a mesh shopping bag, a little girl with an ice cream . . . I heard a roar and shuddered. Vova was clutching his head, crawling on all fours and screaming. Some guy in baggy pants was lashing him with a chain.

"What's wrong with you?"

The twelve-year-old kid was standing beside me, staring hard into my face. Just a little kid like any other. Scruffy, short hair, in a T-shirt with the words "Fuck the stupid chicks" on it. He had such bright, innocent eyes. I felt like some old woman full of wisdom and experience. I said grandly: "You little bastards." Then I thought a moment and said it again. "Bastards. And assholes."

Twenty against one's not right; never. He may be some loser I couldn't give a shit about, but it's the principle of the thing.

The boy squeezed his lips together and thought for a while, then answered brightly:

"Him and his mob fucked Denya over. He split Denya's head open . . ."

"All the same . . ." I said, trying to smooth things over.

"What's all the same? What's it to you?"

Calm down, I thought. No one's going to beat me up; quite the opposite, they're just giving me the eye.

I shrugged.

The tall rapper came over to us, jangling his chain.

"Hi!" he said in a low voice.

Aha . . . His ears stick out from under his cap, a sharp face, mischievous eyes, brazen. Beautiful hands, the hands are something else. I like the hands.

"Right then, comrades," I said, squeezing my way between the little guy and the rapper. The beautiful hands instantly barred my way.

"Where do you live?"

"Zhenya Egorova Street."

The rapper opened his eyes wide and laughed. But he kept on standing there like a traffic barrier, with his arms spread wide.

"That's fucking far away, Nigger," the little kid announced gleefully.

"Give me your number," the rapper said to me, not listening to him.

I shrugged again and rattled off my number. The quicker you tell them, the quicker they lay off you. Nigger wrote the number on his hand and gave me back my pen.

"Denya lives there; he'll see her home," Nigger answered the kid confidently, maintaining the siege.

Half an hour later my ears were popping on the metro, and sitting there beside me staring into empty space was Denya, the one whose head Vova had put a hole in. The scar was clearly visible—stitched up and daubed with bright green ointment. Denya was like Ryan Gosling in *The Believer*. The same shaved head, eyes bunched together, straight nose, beaky lips. But on the whole not too bad, pretty tasty. At least he didn't come on to me. My nerves were already stretched worrying about my bare legs and skintight T-shirt. You can never tell.

Denya took me home without speaking, flashed his hand by way of goodbye and went back the same way. I leapt into the entrance, noting for the hundredth time out of the corner of my eye the words "WU-TANG Clan" on the wall.

"Ilya phoned," my mother informed me. "And how many more times do I have to tell you? It's night outside, and you're wandering around God knows where! Don't let me have to tell you again!" She was gradually limbering up, warming herself up with her own indignation. "No more of these Ilyas."

I closed the door of the room and switched on the computer. While it was churning away I dialed the number.

"Yes?" answered Lyapa.

"Did you call?"

"Yes."

"I'm home."

"That's good. Call me sometime. We've got a gig at Milk soon. I'll take you."

"Okay."

"Later?"

"Later."

I put the phone down. Oh sugar, Lyapa! How long can you carry on being such a dead fish? Or not dead, just not interested in me. How come? Most guys come running if I just throw them one of those lingering looks. But I keep on looking and looking at Lyapa and it's all just a waste of time. He sits there, smokes, looks the other way. At rehearsals they're all falling over each other to amuse me and he just drums away to himself, ignoring me. Once he cut his finger on a torn cymbal. There was blood pouring down onto his dark green shorts; he was sucking furiously at the cut, getting blood on the wall. The drums were streaked with it. I sat there, wondering if I should give him my handkerchief. Volkova was nudging me with her elbow—go on, give it to him. But . . . it didn't seem right somehow, I just couldn't do

it, I don't know why. He didn't look at me. I suppose he
didn't want any handkerchiefs from me.

They began screeching gleefully in the earphones: *"Keep
on lighting up, never take a break, have fun and hang out all night long.
Do drink and funny powders, tell that school so long."*

That's about Lyapa. True, he doesn't do drugs, but he
drinks like a stallion and he's always lighting up; never takes
a break, hangs out all day and all night when they have concerts.

Some day he'll be famous, and I'll be there pointing—
look, that's my husband. He made a real effort at first to get
my attention on the Net, sent me e-mails every day with
"MISS YOU" in huge letters and heaps of exclamation
marks. Now here I am stuck in real life, trying to wake him
up. Trying to make him realize I want that rapid-rush start
to our relationship to continue. Sugar, it's like the Stork and
the Heron . . . He smokes. And looks the other way. Drinks
beer. And looks the other way. Plays the drums like a ma-
niac. And all the time it's like I don't exist for him. Then
why does he ask me to call? Why did he take me to Peterhof
with Volkova and Kres? We had a great time there, climbed
in all the fountains, and a militiaman even tried to chase us.
And in the last fountain it was slippery, and Lyapa took hold
of my hand. Or I took hold of his. I don't remember. And
we stood there under the clear streams of water, squeezing
each other's hands, and all around us everything was bright
and happy. Lyapa's spikes ran and his whole head was covered in gel. We stood there holding hands, and Volkova
couldn't get it together to take a picture of us. Finally she
clicked the shutter and we headed back, still holding hands.
And that was all. Separate again. And we're still separate
now. We walk separately, and it's all just "nothing but."

"*. . . Always writing hits so the brothers will get the feel. No garbage and no drivel and no strife.*"

The telephone rang. I started and looked at the clock— whoa! One o'clock in the morning!

"Hippolet?" Volkova's voice mocked me tenderly in the receiver.

"Whalelet?"

"Guess where I'm calling from!!!"

I listened. Besides Volkova's sniffling into the receiver I could hear the distant rumble of music.

"From a club?"

"Right! And guess what phone I'm using!"

"A mobile."

Somehow I guessed all the answers very quickly. Volkova lost interest in her game and started telling me things in her everyday voice:

"I've met this guy. Thirty-eight. Rich as Croesus . . . . He gave me a lift home from work, then we went to a bar, and then came here. Tarasova's here too. Her guy's worse! Ha ha!"

"Well, naturally," I said with a nod, although Volkova couldn't see me.

"And where did you get to, mush?" Volkova asked, suddenly taking an interest in me.

"I was at Lyapa's place."

"Ah . . . I see," said Volkova. She rattled on, without listening to me. "All right then, Hippolet, I'll call you tomorrow from work. See ya!"

"Yeah, see you."

Volkova enjoys putting me down, but she can't live without me. She likes to be the center of attention, to use a man, to sleep with him (she calls that the "overhead") and then spend ages telling absolutely everyone in glorious Technicolor what she ate, what she drank, what a cool car it was and how much it cost, how the guy's an idiot, and how she's so great and so wonderful.

I half listen to her; I'm not interested. I'd die of boredom if I tried to amuse myself that way. Volkova hates me for that. She thinks I miss out on things in life. But she loves me anyway and misses me terribly when she doesn't see me for a long time.

Denya was sitting on a bench, with his hands stuck in his pockets. I came out of the house and my eyes tripped right over him. I stopped.

"Hi," I said cheerfully and he came over to me. "I thought I'd walk you somewhere," he said.

"Go on, walk me then," I said with a shrug and caught myself thinking that just recently I'd been shrugging a lot. Life is getting a bit beyond my ordinary understanding.

Denya walked me to the metro, then thought a bit and saw me all the way to the school. On the way he told me all sorts of interesting things. He was twenty years old. He'd come back from the army in the spring. He'd served in the Taman Division, he'd been in Chechnya, the grunts had shot all his friends one by one right in front of his eyes, and he was left behind. Now he worked as a security guard, but he found the city boring; he found civilian life boring in general. His girlfriend hadn't waited for him to get out of the army. She was married now. Finally Denya spelled out at length that he thought he really ought to go back to Chechnya.

I was against it. I liked Denya. I don't know why. His eyes were filled with this incredible fuck-it-all disdain for everything.

No matter what happened to the world, he'd just watch, stick his hands in his pocket and go about his own business. It was hard to really get at him. Wish I could be more like that. I tried a fuck-it-all attitude for a whole day, and I was actually very successful at it. Anyway, I skipped Russian language class with a light heart—it was dictation.

Denya was waiting for me by the Kazan Cathedral, sitting on a bench, looking indifferent. He smiled. I beamed back. And we went for a walk.

That evening Volkova came around, fuming with indignation.

"Where've you been all day, fluffhead?" she asked angrily, making herself comfortable on my bed with a bottle of beer and switching on the television. "Put *The Simpsons* on for me. I called you over and over again today."

"We went for a walk."

"Who's 'we'?"

"Me and Denya. Yesterday I was walking from Lyapa's place and I met this boy. He lives not far from here."

Volkova listened impatiently and immediately began recounting the details of how she had spent the previous evening, moving smoothly on into the night and then just as smoothly into the morning.

"The money he has—shit! A BMW. He kept babbling all the time: 'Ah, Lena, I could go on looking at you forever!' He bought me a striptease for a thousand. And then we went to his place, and Tarasova and her friend slept on the floor, because there's only one bed. He's got a prick like a baseball bat! Like that! He drove me back to work in the morning, took my number."

"Will he turn up again?"

"I don't know," Volkova answered lightly. "What about your Denya? Is he a good kisser?"

"I don't know; I haven't tried," I confessed.

Volkova scratched her cheek skeptically, and suggested, "Let's go out somewhere, quick."

We set out for the Fat Man café—we were all dolled up, in high heels, brilliant and beautiful altogether—but halfway there someone called to us:

"Stop! Don't move!"

Volkova stopped, puzzled, staring at a group of kids not far away. Denya came walking toward us, smiling.

"Hello."

"Hi!" I said, delighted.

"Hi," Volkova said coldly, making it clear with every little piece of her that what she deserved was applause, expensive cars and flowers, and not greetings from some juvenile. That's how she thinks of all men under the age of twenty-six without a car. The car maketh the man. Gives him some substance.

Meanwhile all the others had come across too: some boys I didn't know, a girl with a head like an egg with light hair plastered all over it, and Nigger, the guy with the chain. This didn't suit Volkova's plans, so she spent the rest of the evening with a sour face.

We strolled out to Ozerki and back, drank some beer and then went to the park on the other side of the railway line, and Denya's crowd began singing songs. They lit a bonfire. A girl sang in a squeaky voice, *This is the world, I live here. You and our friends all live here too . . .* and plonked away on a guitar. Little Misha with the broad shoulders attached himself to Volkova. I sat opposite them on a bench. Denya took the guitar.

"Why do you stare at me that way? I'm not yours anymore. In two years I've met lots of boys."

I got up and went behind some kind of bush, because the beer was bursting out of me. Then I went back and saw a figure in wide pants a little distance away from the group. It was Nigger.

"Hi there again," I said way too merrily, ogling him with drunken eyes.

In the dark forms melt, melt into the darkness. My lips seek other lips, but I know they're not the ones . . .

I don't remember how it all happened, but the next minute I was in Nigger's arms and he was breathing into my face with his mouth open. Then he kissed me. My brain stalled for a moment, then went into a spin. Nigger was strong and nice to touch, like a young horse. His eyes shone with a mixture of insolence and childishness and with a farewell gurgle I drowned in them. We kept on kissing until Misha came across us on his way to take a piss. Misha said a polite "Oh!" and moved away. Nigger and I stared at each other, drunk and stunned, then went back to the bonfire.

Volkova, the insolent cow, understood everything at once. She kept winking at me, meaningfully. And Denya went on singing song after song as though nothing had happened, all of them mournful soldier's tunes—everyone in the whole wide world's abandoned me and all that stuff. But his eyes were still full of disdain. I know I couldn't be like that all the time. I couldn't just not give a shit about anything, because I don't know any place I could hide. But Denya knows one—behind all his dead friends. They were here, then they were gone. Right in front of him. That's why his eyes are so empty.

He sang and looked at me. And I looked at him. And I thought: My head's *really* fucked up!

I got home late again. And she started up again: "How many more times? It's dark outside, and you're wandering around God knows where! Don't let it happen again!" I nodded. What else could I do? I couldn't promise I really would come back early. I wasn't going to.

Nothing but brazen lies and crazy raving,
Nothing but dust and vainest vanity,
Nothing but a broken string still screaming.
In this world our dreams are all we see . . .
Dreams dreamed about nothing,
Dreams for the sake of dreaming

Denya was sitting on the bench outside, hunched over, staring into a bush. I remembered with a sober mind everything that had happened the day before and I thought: Uh-oh . . .

He stood up and said only, "Hi. I'll walk you."

Nigger was there in front of my eyes through all my lectures that day. I had this unsettling feeling, as though I'd lost something important and I really had to get it back. Or else . . . Or else what? I don't know. Nigger lives in the Southwest District. That's an hour from me by metro. And Denya's right here; he even walks me to classes.

He's there by the Kazan Cathedral again. I spotted him from a distance and immediately turned into the metro. I jumped over the turnstile; the alarm started screeching furiously. No one chased me. No one ever chases anyone. Lyapa taught me how to ride the metro without paying.

I got home and clocked the words "WU-TANG Clan" in the entrance again. I sat down on the bed and started thinking about what I ought to do. The telephone rang.

"Is this the student residence hall? Can you call Liudochka, please," a voice lisped in the receiver.

"Oh!" I exclaimed happily. "Volkova! You're just the person I need. I've got a problem!"

"Fallen in love with the rapper, have you?" Volkova guessed gleefully.

"How can I find him?"

"Easy. Let's go for another walk with that sicko Denya. Seems to me like he left all his marbles back in Chechnya. You'll get to hug and squeeze your man there."

"He might not come! He lives in the Southwest District."

"If he doesn't come, we'll ask for his number. From someone in the group." Volkova was pleased with herself, happy to be so quick-witted about giving me advice.

"Okay. Only you ask for the number. I'm too shy."

"Okay, little Hippolet," said Volkova. "But is Liudmilochka there?"

"You know, she's taking a bath. Ah, here she is, toweling herself off already!"

Nigger wasn't there. But the egg-girl was. And so was Denya. We were sitting in the Fat Man, drinking beer. Denya was buying. He was having fun and was beautiful in his disdain and generosity. Volkova kept looking around for some man so she could give him a look and then amuse herself by fighting off his advances. I was on hot coals. I wanted to jump up and run, run, run, shouting out at the top of my voice to spew this monstrous impatience from inside me.

Volkova finally responded to my despairing glances. She

waited until Denya and Misha went to the bathroom and asked the egg-girl with feigned indifference:

"That guy . . . what's his name . . . with the oversized pants."

"Pasha!"

"Ah, yes, Pasha . . . Do you know his phone number? My brother wants to talk to him about some business or other."

It was really smart of Volkova to make up the story about her brother. The girl rummaged in her handbag and even found a sheet of paper and wrote the number on it for Volkova: "Pavel, 142–34–75."

Volkova thanked her and stuck the paper in her pocket. Misha and Denya came back. They separated to see us home: Misha with Volkova, Denya with me and the egghead. Somehow the girl disappeared quickly. Denya took hold of my hand. He led me as far as the entrance. Stood there looking in my eyes, then put his arms round me and tried to kiss me. I wriggled free like a lizard, fluttered my eyelashes guiltily and smiled. I flew into the elevator without even noticing the words on the wall as I passed them. Then I stood on the third floor for a long time, waiting for Denya to go away.

Ten minutes later I was ringing the doorbell of Volkova's apartment. She came out half undressed, with a wide yawn. Handed me the piece of paper.

"What would you do without me?" she asked pompously, and then immediately dropped her languorous expression:

"You wouldn't believe how long it took me to fight off that Misha! I'm damned if I'm going out with those idiots again!"

"Damned if I am too," I responded automatically.

*　*　*

My mother started harassing me again, and I realized it was late and it wouldn't be decent to call Nigger.

On the one hand, that is.

But on the other hand I missed him. My soul felt sort of empty, but at the same time cluttered with junk. Everything was all over the place. I wanted to take a broom and a dustpan and sweep out everything I didn't need, clean off everything I did and set it all out neatly on the shelves. There's Denya, there's Nigger. Throw this one out, stand that one on the shelf. Or the other way around.

Nigger picked up the phone. I got flustered and didn't say anything.

"Who is it?" he asked.

"It's me."

"Hmm . . . Who exactly?"

Then I remembered Nigger didn't know my name. Then who am I? Where am I? Why am I? Er, er, er . . . What an idiot. I called him.

"Ah! It's you!" Nigger suddenly guessed somehow, and said "you" in a voice that made it clear he meant me.

"How are you doing?" I inquired casually. Okay, it's a cliché, but I can't just say straight out, "I missed you." We've only known each other two days, and even then not really.

"All right," Nigger replied. "And you?"

"I'm all right too." I paused. "Why didn't you come today?"

"It's a long way!" he said cheerfully.

Everything collapsed. My mood, the corners of my mouth, even my arms almost dropped off. Papier-mâché. Tap it once and it breaks. A long way! It's a long way for him to come to me! So the district is what decides things. So there can't be anything between us . . . "A long way . . ." I didn't want to talk anymore. My throat felt so tight I could hardly squeeze out the words: "Okay, bye then."

"Okay . . . bye," said Nigger, surprised.

I hung up. What do I want with the Southwest District? I have Denya. Yes, I do. He's all right. He's good-looking . . . I started trying to persuade myself. Superficially I did. But he really was good-looking. And he'd come back from the war. "Left all his marbles behind." Volkova's right. He doesn't understand humor. He smokes and stares into space. He sings songs as though he's rubbing your nose in it: "A girl should be faithful. I'm a soldier; I defended the borders of the homeland. All the others are just jerks . . . And I have a right to love." He does. But mine?

The next evening I was sitting in Denya's kitchen with my head propped on my hands examining his army photographs. We'd had a few drinks and everything was swimming in front of my eyes. Denya, naked from the waist up, was smoking, leaning out of the window. On his left shoulder there was a naked woman and the word "Taman." On his right shoulder were some patterns. And the photographs: there's Denya without any tattoos, and there he is with "Taman" already. There's his mom and dad, there he is festooned with submachine guns. His friends. His friends again. An armored car.

Denya flicked the butt out into the darkness and sat down on a stool.

"If there wasn't war then there wouldn't be the heaviest thing of all, the thing you need so you can wrap your nerves tight around your fist," he said. "So the blood can flow, not out of little scratches, but in streams . . . out of wounds . . . with the flesh torn open . . ."

And clear eyes, I thought. Iron, smoke, foul language and all the time those clear eyes. Yours. *"And you can't fight your friend, if you don't, if you don't, if you don't have a friend!"* . . . If you're not alive . . . Am I alive?

"To die—for something really big," Denya continued with his thought. "With no filth, just all one big piece. But we keep on fiddling away with some stupid lump of plasticine. What for? I want to go to war. Get killed there. That's what I fucking want."

"And what will I do?"

At that moment it really seemed to me that if he went away to war I'd be left frozen by the window in a prison of grief.

"You'll go on living," said Denya, coming over all brave and gallant. "You'll find yourself a decent young guy, not all fucked up like me," he said, enjoying putting himself down.

It's always the way. Men naturally exaggerate so they can hear you answer: "No, you're wrong. You're fantastic." And I answered:

"What would I want with a decent young man?"

Denya let my outburst go, absorbed in his own thoughts.

"In the army and in prison, that's where things are real. That's where you can see what a man's really like . . . Without all that—fuck it—self . . . self-expression. You're all alone face-to-face with yourself in there. And it's not a matter of soldiers and grunts."

"Of what then?"

"People. The little mama's boys are every fucking place now. All sorts of stuck-up wimps who hide behind daddy—you try going one-on-one with me, fucker, then we'll see

who's really hard. I couldn't give a fuck how hard the bastard is . . . He hasn't seen any real death, when your friends
are ripped into mincemeat beside you. Useless idle
fuckers . . . rich bastards. Fuck them all, every one of them.
Put the fucking bunch in the army."

I looked hard at Denya, but he didn't see me; his eyes
were full of idle fuckers and his friends. His friends were obviously shafting the idle fuckers with mop handles. Or
submachine-gun barrels.

I had trouble waking up.

I didn't feel dizzy, but I still had those pleasant vestiges
of tiredness, when you don't get enough sleep because of
something that's important to you. I sat on the bed and
pieced together a picture of the evening before. There was
a kitchen, cigarettes, a park, Denya's kisses, illogical and
somehow exactly right. Who is he to me? That's the question. But simply . . . no, not simply. It's complicated.
Everything went straight to my head; everything just came
together the way it had to, like the only correct answer out
of all those warm, sunny answers carefully thought out in
every detail. Wham, and that's it. There is something to
him. Inside. And outside. His back too, the scar on his
shaved head . . . and the tattoos. How good it is that I have
Denya. How good that he's here with me. Only a few days,
but it seemed longer.

Volkova called.

"You filthy bitch," she began abusing me, but then
changed her mind and got to the point: "There's a gig at
Milk today. Lyapa the Flapper called and said we should

come up to the Griboedov Canal, if we want." (Volkova emphasized the words as though we might not want to.)

"What time's the gig?"

"What's it matter what time?" Volkova prattled on, disgruntled. "We have to be there at five, so afterward they can get ready without getting nervous. Why don't I go straight to the Gribanal from work; we finish early today."

"Okay, I'll come."

"Of course you will!!! How're you getting along with Nigger?" she said as an afterthought.

"Er, er . . ." I faltered.

"Okay then, see you this evening, darling." Volkova clearly didn't have time to wait for me to get my thoughts together.

"Bye."

Volkova couldn't give a shit. She's going to Milk for free booze and to be entertained. To watch the drunken girls wanting Lyapa, Kres, Sam and Vitya. She's even less interested in them than in me. I'm the one who sits at Lyapa's place and burns my tongue with coffee, not her.

Then why does Lyapa phone Volkova, and not me? Hmm.

I thought: Lyapa's only eighteen, he hasn't been in the army . . . He doesn't know life.

Lyapa played as though he was born with drumsticks in his hands. Volkova had put away some beer at Milk and now she was relaxed, contemplating the crowd, and over their heads fat-cheeked Sam with his tongue sticking out and his bass guitar sticking out too. Vitya the lead guitarist, dark-

skinned, with thick black bangs. Kres yelling into the microphone. Right over by the wall the glittering cymbals, the
flickering drumsticks and Lyapa's sweaty face.

She hurries on barefoot . . . along the road from heaven . . .
But the stones wound her feet . . . and the road has no end

In my gut everything was rumbling and roaring. The
music had pierced me to the core. None of my own thoughts
were left, and the joy was blazing in my eyes. I was transparent, nothing else to me.

Volkova had crazy, loving eyes. And her eyebrows curved
elegantly.

I wandered around with a glass of beer. Lyapa licked his
lips feverishly, drank some mineral water out of a plastic bottle, stared at Vitya. Vitya began slowly, rhythmically, almost
syllable by syllable.

Your half-closed eyes explained to me just why
The drunken wind fanned war's old embers into flames
There's a reason for the flames that scorch across the sky
I whisper foolish words, a captive to my hopeless dreams

Then Kres began in a hoarse voice:

Give! Me! Give! Me! Give! Me! A little sunshine!!!
Give! Me! Give! Me! Give! Me! A little water!!!

The crowd began jumping up and down, the energy just
pouring out of every one of them, and I nearly went mad
with happiness. It was that happiness you get at a gig; every-

thing around me was a single whole, it was running through everyone: "Give! Me! Give! Me!!! Aaaagh!!!"

Nothing else matters.

Afterward we went over to Sam's place. Got drunk as pigs. The last thing I remember was Volkova's calling me "my sweet little girl." Sam and some woman are collapsing on the divan and dark-skinned Vitya's getting the woman undressed in anticipation.

In the morning I find out that while I was at Milk having fun, "some skinhead came around. Who is he? Is he the one you stay out with late at night?" That's clear enough then; Denya's discovered he's in love with me. Or something like that.

After yesterday's wild turn-on at Milk, Denya seemed old-fashioned, like someone who doesn't know how to have fun. Out of style. But who's in style? Some guy who doesn't know real life? Inside me everything was singing and roaring. I couldn't give a shit about anything. Life is beautiful and amazing. *"Nothing but brazen lies and crazy raving, Nothing but dust and vainest vanity."* Lyapa deserves a good smack in the head, the idiot, for not wanting me. Yes, finish him off! *"Hey mama, it feels so good!!!"*

At the peak of my high the phone rang and Nigger's voice at the other end of the line was perfect. He got right to the point and said:

"Is that you? Let's go out for a walk."

"Yes!" I thought. And he answered quickly:

"I'll come over. Let's meet by the escalator in an hour."

"Yes, let's!"

This is the picture: I'm standing there watching the escalator, and out comes this tall rapper in a light-colored "NY" cap with Dumbo ears, brazen eyes and a big smile plastered right across his face. Big wide shoulders, fit as a stallion. He's riding up, and it seems to take forever. Oh, finally! He's coming over to me. Under a yellow checked shirt he has a white T-shirt and below that he has wide pants with a dangling chain. I tried not to think about the fact that this chain once lashed a certain Vova around the head.

It's the first time I've seen Nigger with sober eyes and in daylight. He turned out to be a whole head taller than me. That's important, because normally the boys are at best the same height as me. If I really try I can rest my arm on Lyapa's head. Especially when I'm in high heels.

"Hi!" said Nigger happily. "Hi, kitten!"

I felt proud to have him beside me. We rode in the metro and I looked at him from his feet to his head and smiled like some American tourist. Then we walked down Nevsky Prospect and I accepted numerous ice creams from him, until finally I was so full I needed to go dashing off somewhere. We turned into Palace Square and took a look at the tumbling break-dancers. Sat down not far away in a park by a fountain, and got some beer. There were children and tourists splashing in the fountain.

Nigger told me about rap, and sang: *"I don't believe my ears, I don't believe my eyes—hip-hop's been handed over to a bunch of shitty guys."* Then he got embarrassed. Looked at me with his brazen eyes and kissed me.

The children squealed for joy. The tourists clicked away with their cameras.

"We gotta make a change . . ."

Everything fell into place. The mess inside my head was replaced with neat, tidy shelves. It's all simple—*no garbage and no drivel and no strife.* Except there was still one cupboard in there that had been hastily crammed with thoughts about war and prison, about sweaty boys and hoarse voices . . .

I've stopped going over to Volkova's place. Either I get home late or I forget. Volkova isn't offended, especially since right now she's involved with a rich man and she's been doing the rounds of tourist spots and kebab-houses with him.

We were sitting on the embankment with our legs dangling. Steamers and speedboats with tourists sailed this way and that way. We'd chosen a good spot so tourists who wanted to snap the Winter Palace from a speedboat had to snap us as well. True, in the photos we'd be the size of flies. But it's still a nice feeling.

"Maybe I should dress normally," Nigger suddenly said out of nowhere, looking straight in front of him.

"Meaning?"

"Meaning like a meathead. Narrow jeans, T-shirt . . ."

Nigger twisted his thin lips so I could scarcely see them. Inside, the thought must have seemed okay. But as soon as he said it he changed his mind. "Shit, that's really bad."

"What brought that on?"

"You know, everybody just pisses me off. They all think, hey, DMC—great! Then there's guys in baggy pants all over the place. If you're gonna wear the clothes, then you gotta know rap. And not just because it's in fashion now." Nigger clenched his fists militantly. "Above all, it's rap culture. Or else, every fucker will listen to Eminem or, even worse, DMC, and put on the baggy pants—like, we're real hard rappers . . . And I've been going around like this for four years now; been listening to rap for five. And it drives me wild when some dmc walks up and looks at me like I'm a friend of his, like he's the same as me . . . When he's just some thick meathead and he could never fucking match up to me."

"Oh!" was all I could think of to say.

Nigger roused himself.

"Oh, kitten. There I go spouting shit! I'm sorry."

"Why is it shit? You're not a meathead, are you? Screw 'em all."

"That's right!" Nigger stuck out his chest, put his arm around me, pressed his cold cheek against mine: "Kitten, oh kitten!"

"What?"

"I love you!"

Pain squeezes at my temples like it wants me dead.
I wanted to make steps, but I got stuck halfway there,

I can't tell what this madness is bursting my sick head . . .
What are these words? Who'll show me what the meaning is
and where?

"Hippolet?"

"Whalelet!"

Volkova and I finally met up and we celebrated the occasion. We celebrated at Volkova's place, with mugs of gin. Outside the darkness was warm, and inside the lamp glowed, the fridge gurgled and the drink glugged out of the bottle. As usual, I felt drawn to unburden my heart. Volkova got swept away in the same storm. And we sat in the kitchen with our legs pulled in under our stools, not listening to each other. Sharing. Between the Hippolet and the Whalelet.

"That rapper, sugar! Doesn't want to listen to anything except his rap. Okay, let him have rap. But I can't even mention Zemfira any more. He just says—it's crap!" I complained artistically.

"What an idiot!" Volkova dismissed him and carried on with her own line. "And mine says: 'My wife doesn't satisfy me!' Ha! Fucker. So I said I wanted to go to . . . that expensive place . . . Well, shit me! Anyway, we went! And he laid out five grand! For dinner!" Volkova's eyes open wide.

I thought she'd overdone it. Why be so quick to call Nigger an idiot? I decided to throw in a few positive points.

"He doesn't really mind Zemfira . . . And anyway I'm no great fan . . . you've seen my MP3s; I listen to a bit of everything . . . And he always walks me home and hangs out on the bench with me. Sometimes till two in the morning. God knows how he gets home afterward. All the way to Southwest District!"

"You callous cow!" Volkova screamed, insulting me. "The metro's closed then! So, then he drove me back, see, to the apartment." Volkova pensively pours me some gin. "Not the one he shares with the wife. The one he rents. Not bad, the furniture's okay. With a TV. And a video . . . But his prick's not so great." Volkova giggles into her mug. "I almost laughed out loud in bed. What a joke!"

"Nothing but long forgotten old birdsong! Nothing but the gaze of empty eyes! And all those things we lived for for so very long—all of the world today—oh, dreams! . . . Dreams dreamed about nothing, dreams for the sake of dreaming!"

Volkova's Rottweiler came in and looked at us, puzzled. At two drunken faces.

I've been lucky in life. I didn't go to any extra classes after school, but then I got into the arts program, just like that. My teachers couldn't believe it. A "C" student, neither fish nor fowl, as far as they were concerned I was no success story—and then the arts program! Even the top students failed the exams and went around with their eyes all red from crying. But I passed them, and kept a straight face. Acted as though I wasn't even pleased about it.

I didn't exactly get the best catch. But what washed ashore was all mine. In the first year the star student Sakharov washed up. Everyone loved him, and he loved me. At first it was mutual; then after a year and a half I got fed up. Sakharov wore white shirts and twill trousers. Shirt and twill every day. The pants are worn till they're worn out; they hang off his backside like a parachute. But he knows every Socrates and Shakespeare there is to know of by heart. What good are they to me? I wanted beer and sex in unlimited quantities, not just during the five minutes before Sakharov's mother arrived. I heard a song with the words: *"It's too late to think about anything, I can feel I need some air. We're living in the middle of a swamp . . ."* and I decided it was time for the "forgive me, my love" speech. Everyone threw his or her hands up in dismay. Sakharov stayed home for months, like a ghost.

To replace Sakharov, Yashnikov from the fifth year came floating ashore. Sturdy, blond, gorgeous smile. Everyone loved Yashnikov too, but he didn't love anyone. I got hurt and cried into my pillow. Then one day Andrei appeared on the horizon and Yashnikov drowned somewhere or other, I don't know where. Unlike Sakharov and Yashnikov, Andrei had nothing to do with the arts program. He worked as a security guard and shaved his head. And he didn't quite drift ashore; he floated past my shell-strewn beach, flashed his hand and I thought: I'll take that one. I love him. Can't help myself. Andrei thought differently: I will, then I will again, but after that . . . We met right through the autumn. Twice a week. It's absolutely great! It's Andrei! More perfect than perfect! Six years older. Knows absolutely nothing about linguistics. But he has his own philosophy: "Screw every sucker and enjoy it" and "Maul the fuckers." Fuckers meant everyone except girls and friends. That criminal romance had my head spinning. For a while, that is.

Andrei put an end to us, and it was my turn to be a ghost. I crept around in misery. Volkova couldn't understand—what the fuck was he doing inside my head?

Andrei stayed there for a long time, almost a year. Meanwhile Sakharov had found himself a girl and dumped her again. He walked around sticking out his skinny little chest. I suspected that in that chest love for me was still stirring, but I didn't say so out loud. Sakharov was pathologically sensitive. He immersed himself in study, pulling up the pants that he'd worn into a droopy parachute backside. Sometimes he looked at me tenderly. To be honest, I was thinking: maybe I should go back, take a rest beside him . . . In any case there was no one floating ashore anymore. Andrei was a snake. And there was no one else in all the world . . .

Lyapa floated in at the end of the epic with Andrei. Wrote all sorts of funny letters, like "hugs and kisses, your Turnip." My turnip. Mine?

And now there was Nigger. I was blown away. I thought they didn't make them like that anymore.

But it turned out they do.

Nigger expresses his opinion of my previous passions like this: "jerk," "idiot," "a slob." I can't understand anymore why I wasted so much time on all those Andreis. And that Sakharov—God . . . And Yashnikov is nothing but a tapeworm. We bumped into him at a club, the VMC. Yashnikov came running up to say hello; shook his curls about. Nigger looked down on him from above with a glance of contempt. Almost spat on him.

Lyapa's punk rock, not rap. But even if Nigger liked punk rock, he'd never listen to songs by my "husband." The boy's jealous. "Even if you put Zemfira on, I'd say she was better than this . . . Lyapa."

It all seems clear enough.

* * *

Six months have gone by.

I don't see Denya anymore. I don't know where he is. Perhaps he's gone to Chechnya. Perhaps he's snowed under with work. Perhaps, as Volkova says, he's gotten married. At least that would be something.

I love Nigger. I become terribly boring when the conversation is about Nigger.

Misery, that's all people want to hear about—everybody's curious to learn all the well-worn details. Happiness is banal. It's the same for everyone. It's a waste of time talking about it. They won't understand; and it's boring.

Volkova's grown her hair and lost six pounds. Now she arrives back at the house in jeeps, all high and mighty and dolled up. The neighbors gasp, call her "a whore" behind her back and are all sweetness and light to her face. The neighbors aren't as beautiful as Volkova. That's clear enough. Volkova's become conceited. But I know she's just a whalelet.

I haven't seen Lyapa for the whole six months.

And now it's spring. Everything's flowering and smelling good.

I set off for Nigger's place in the Southwest District and run into my "husband" on the metro. He hasn't changed, still good-looking in the same puppy-dog way. His eyes gleam playfully; his lips stretch uncontrollably into a lazy, guilty smile. His shoulders are held high—maybe because they're holding up a knapsack, or maybe it's embarrassment. The weather's cool, but he doesn't have a cap. He has horns on his head.

"Kitten!" he says loudly and happily, with his eyes wandering off to one side of me . . .

So there we were, sitting in the same old kitchen again. The rest of the group was going crazy in the other room.

Sam and Kres were tearing each other's heads off, and Vitya was playing GTA2. Swearing like a trooper. The cops kept catching him every five minutes, you see. So it was a gnarly game.

Everyone was drunk after the rehearsal. But Lyapa wasn't far gone yet.

"What do you want, coffee?"

"Give me beer, you freak . . ."

He was delighted and opened me a Petrovskoe with a deafening pop.

I looked at my husband and thought: idiot punk. Funny. Foolish. Look at him, a husband. And mine too. Should I get divorced, then?

"Lyapa let's, you know, get divorced!" I joked awkwardly.

"What for?" he said, startled. "Are you fed up with me?"

"Fed up?" We hadn't seen each other for six months.

"You don't really care," I answered quickly and took a hasty gulp of beer.

Lyapa's eyes looked different. He wasn't looking to one side, but straight at me. He didn't understand. Was I joking? There didn't seem to be any of the usual mockery. What then? He didn't understand, didn't understand, didn't understand. Then he understood.

"I simply didn't think you could be interested in me at all . . ."

My jaw dropped down to the floor. He "didn't think"! How come?

"Why didn't you?" I asked.

"Because I'm a little, stupid, ugly punk."

It was funny. No one but Lyapa could beg for compliments as openly as that. Lyapa the Flapper. Simple and complicated in a single wrapper. He's bright and happy, but what's inside him? Nothing but "Give! Me! Give! Me! Give! Me! A little sunshine"? Would you believe it—"an ugly punk."

"I'm not fishing for compliments," he said, realizing he'd overplayed it a touch. "Maybe I'm exaggerating, of course, but basically that's how it is."

Sam came in and rummaged around noisily in the fridge, and smirked at the sight of me and of Lyapa sitting there goggle-eyed. Went out.

Lyapa stood up; I thought he'd follow Sam out. And that's all right, Nigger's waiting for me after all. But Lyapa closed the kitchen door and turned toward me.

"I love you, kitten."

"What?"

Lyapa forced his way through his embarrassment as if it were barbed wire, cast off his idiotic expression, so his face became plain and tense, and moved up close to me, breathing heavily.

"Er . . . er . . . Lyapa . . ."

"No more messing around," he said seriously.

Suddenly his tongue was in my mouth.

valerochka

They boarded the train in a more or less organized fashion. Lidia checked the head count, mothers wiped away the tears and in some cases eyeliner, fathers squeezed hands, slapped shoulders and told their children to keep their chins up.

The smaller kids pressed their noses against the windows, wrinkling up their little eyebrows and shouting "Bye, mom!" The older ones strolled up and down the canvas runners, glancing into the open compartments, sizing each other up and whiling away the time. Stasik Galkin cried quietly; he didn't want to go to any summer camp anymore, and he couldn't care less anymore about the mysterious ocean.

Lidia gently took hold of his hand, led him over to the window and whispered: "We'll write mommy letters. We'll bring her a beautiful shell, and she'll be really pleased!" Stasik scratched his nose and waved uncertainly in the direction of the platform.

Couplings clanged, wheels turned and parents, platform and station started gliding backward. The children jostled in the corridor, taking a last look at the town, and then went to their compartments.

Olesya changed and stuck her bag under the seat. She smiled politely at the three girls on the other bunks in the compartment. They smiled back, looking frightened. Then they all introduced themselves. Olesya went out of the compartment and leaned against the handrail. Trees flashed by in front of her eyes, sometimes dropping down below the track, sometimes soaring up above it. The sun blinked brightly through the leaves. Stasik stood at the next window, staring at the blind.

The wheels hammered out a regular rhythm; there was a smell of hot rails and Chinese noodles. Olesya heard someone singing:

I'll fuck over any ugly cunt or jerk-off,
I'll shaft the junkies with their needles and their grass,
Pay back each look that's even slightly crooked
That comes my way from any slick smart-ass.
My life's all gym and sex and milk.
I don't take put-downs from any bitch.
You, with your stink of booze and smokes, you sleazy
Lowlife, step out, and I'll fuck you over easy!

The voice belonged to a boy of about thirteen. He waved his hands around as he sang, his eyes focused intensely. The two boys sitting beside him and listening were a bit older.

One was wearing track pants, naked from the waist up, with a gold chain, hair that stood on end and a freckly face. The other had curly hair and was wearing a sports shirt two sizes too big and oversize jeans too.

All three of them turned their heads to look at Olesya when she came to the doorway. The expression of interest on her face was so strong that there was no room left for embarrassment. Stasik peeped out from behind her elbow. Apparently he was the fourth occupant of the compartment.

"Hi," said Olesya.

"Hi," replied the curly-haired one. The thirteen-year-old gave her a hostile look: he was embarrassed because Olesya had surprised him in his moment of inspiration.

"I'm sorry," Olesya said to him. "I heard you and I thought it sounded interesting."

The boy thawed. A smug look appeared in his eyes.

"What sounded so interesting?" he asked, nonchalant.

It turned out his name was Ignat. He had transparent ears that looked like baby's hands set on the sides of his head. His light hair was styled in a crew cut, but it wouldn't stand up, so his head looked like it was covered with fluff that had been sleeked down. He had a sore on his lip. He kept touching it and twitching his nose, sniffing loudly.

The one with the chain was called Taras. Olesya chuckled to herself, Great names they all have. Where did they dig them up from, the dictionary? She wasn't at all surprised when the curly-haired one held out his hand and introduced himself as "Innokentii."

"Curly number one," Taras explained with a laugh.

"Want to play cards with us?" Curly asked.

Olesya guessed that Curly and Taras were old friends, but that Ignat had only met them on the way to the camp.

Curly and Taras obviously weren't the sort to use their friendship as a barrier, to keep other people away. They understood the advantages of their position and invited others to join them with a gesture of almost royal generosity. Olesya agreed to play cards. She liked the look of Curly. And Ignat. And Taras too. But she had no intention of trying to captivate them with her charms. She knew well enough that her short, "plucked-sparrow" haircut, thin-framed glasses and plumpish figure weren't exactly the ideal image for a date.

Stasik squeezed past Olesya into the compartment. His cheeks were still wet with tears. Curly surprised everyone, including himself, by picking Stasik up, sitting him on his knee and saying:

"If anyone bullies you, you tell me."

"I will," promised Stasik.

When Olesya came back into her compartment, the other girls had already made friends and were getting ready for a collective lunch. They'd laid the food out on the little table: noodles, tomatoes, smoked chicken, sausage and biscuits. They were delighted to see Olesya. She rummaged in her bag and added her contribution to the feast: a bunch of bananas, a bottle of Sprite and some bread.

In the evening long lines of kids with towels and toothbrushes lined up for the toilet. Lidia checked that they all had their bedsheets, and gave out strict instructions, telling them not to go out into the corridor unless they really needed to, not to run around, not to make noise and not to smoke.

The train's wheels hammered on the tracks, and the pillowcases and sheets gave off a cold, fresh smell. Olesya lay on the top bunk, watching the lights fly past the window. The other girls were asleep. Olesya felt a sweet ache inside from the coziness of the compartment, the rhythm of the wheels and the smell of the wooden sleepers. The little lamp above the window glowed softly. Traced out in felt-tip pen on the ceiling were the words "Lara and Tanya rode home up here."

Olesya got up quietly and opened the heavy door, moving on tiptoe. The corridor was empty and the curtains were swaying. Lidia's instructions had been obeyed: this time the children were unusually compliant. They were the sons and daughters of factory management staff traveling on special deals, comparatively well-off children who were generally good-natured. Olesya was afraid Lidia or the conductor would turn up at any moment and send her back to bed. So she quickly stole into the lobby at the end of the compartments.

The lobby was cold, and the smell of cigarette smoke and iron hung in the air. Olesya shivered. She wasn't alone: a rather short boy stepped away from the wall toward her.

"Hi," he said.

"Hi."

The boy was wearing a cropped black leather jacket and glasses. His head was shaved. Another "four-eyes" like Olesya.

"Can't sleep?" he inquired.

"You too?" Olesya answered him with a question.

"I like the lobbies on trains," said the boy. "They shake

and rattle, they're drafty and people are always smoking in them. Compartments are too much like being at home. It spoils the fun of traveling."

"It doesn't spoil anything," said Olesya with a shiver. "It's better in the compartment. Up on the top bunk with the view out the window changing all the time. And they rattle and shake too."

"Maybe you're right," the boy agreed.

There was a pause, with the silence punctuated by the rhythm of the wheels.

"Are you going to camp too?" asked Olesya.

"Yes," said the boy, with a nod.

"What's your name?"

"Valerii," he answered, but he didn't ask what Olesya was called.

She felt offended. "Who does he think he is!" she snorted to herself.

Taking no notice of Olesya's scowl, Valerii took a table-tennis ball out of his pocket. The celluloid sphere glowed a milky white in the darkness.

"Look."

Olesya pursed her lips in annoyance, but took a glance out of the corner of her eye anyway. Valerii bounced the little sphere off the floor with a clunk, then swung his arm and flung it at the window. The ball went flying out through the frame. Olesya shuddered in surprise. Why had he thrown it out?

Valerii gave a wide smile, screwing up his eyes with the short little lashes and showing off his rabbit's teeth. Olesya frowned. So now he was delighted with himself for throwing it out? A strange boy.

"Touch it," he said.

"What?" asked Olesya, mystified.

"The glass."

"What glass?"

Valerii took her hand and pressed it against the window through which the little ball had disappeared only a minute before. Her hand came up against cold glass. Olesya ran her palm up and down; the glass was set firmly into its rubber frame.

"But where's the ball?" she asked.

"Gone," Valerii answered gleefully.

That night Olesya dreamed all sorts of inconsequential non-sense—her mother putting her clothes in her bag, then the books off the shelf, then the aquarium, and telling her: "Be sure to dress up warm! Eat lots of fruit! Don't drink water that hasn't been boiled!"

Lidia walked past all the compartments, giving her charges strict instructions to stop messing around and get ready.

An hour later the train stopped at the station and the boys and girls made their way to the exits, chattering loudly. Curly and Ignat dragged Olesya's suitcase along on its wheels and Taras dragged Stasik along with his knapsack. Lidia was feeling nervous, but she tried not to show it. In a thunderous voice she ordered them to line up in columns—and once again the factory children did as they were told, without scattering across the platform, screaming and shouting, the way Lidia's previous groups had done on arrival. She loaded them onto two buses and left Klara Petrova in charge of one. Klara was a severe, responsible fourteen-year-old girl with thick braids and a ring in her nose. She had always been given positions of responsibility. At nursery school she was the teacher's little helper, in charge of checking that the children had washed their hands before they ate. Then later, at school, she had been a better student than anyone else and had performed in all the holiday concerts. She was appointed editor of the little newspaper they posted on the wall and learned the power of the printed word—pupils became good or bad not because of their behavior, but because of what was written about them. Klara wrote the headlines in felt-tip pen. People toadied up to her and wanted to be friends with her. But she tried to be impartial, and that was probably why even Taras Eremeev, the undisputed king of her class, 9B, acknowledged her authority without question.

Now Taras was sitting on the bus behind Klara, his impudent eyes staring into her severe ones through the driving mirror. Klara frowned. Taras wound his chain onto his finger. Olesya was sitting beside Ignat, who was swinging his legs happily and singing to himself: *"My life's all gym and sex and milk . . ."* Olesya secretly wondered if Ignat's life really did include all these components, especially the second, but she said nothing and just smiled to herself. She was looking forward to an ocean of sunshine, happiness, salt sea spray, heaps of translucent grapes and watermelons smelling of snow. As the sun rose over the horizon, lighting up the bus with a dense orange glow, the boys and girls squinted and laughed happily, imagining the same things as Olesya.

* * *

The bus pulled out onto a wide road and little houses started flashing by. At first the passing landscape was interesting, but soon it became monotonous, and Olesya turned her attention to the inside of the bus.

Curly was asleep next to Stasik, and holding a tomato with a bite taken out of it. Taras gazed out of the window with a fixed, vacant stare. The girls Olesya had shared the compartment with were squealing and giggling. Valerii was sitting beside a big girl dressed in a tight-fitting T-shirt that made her look even fatter than she was. His hands were folded on his battered knapsack. Next to the rosy-cheeked, well-nourished girl he looked thin and pale, as if he'd only just thawed out after the winter.

Valerii spotted Olesya and smiled, then started looking out of the window.

Olesya didn't respond. She'd taken a dislike to him back there in the lobby on the train. He was too puny; the way his lips curled and his cheekbones stuck out was ugly; his shaved head, gleaming in the sunshine, made him look like a worm.

A tapeworm, thought Olesya.

Klara announced that they were stopping. The boys and girls began scrambling about. Curly woke up and dropped his tomato.

Olesya was put in a cozy little room for four, with bunk beds. She found herself with Irka Kriukova, a vivacious ginger-haired girl with a throaty voice; Polinka, who smiled sweetly all the time, dressed in lilac and pink; and the fat girl in the tight T-shirt, Olya Kliueva.

Polinka announced in a high, pleasant voice that she was glad to find herself in such "nice company" and that she was certain "we'll all be friends," and everyone immediately relaxed. As if they really had become friends right away. They made up the beds, put their bags away in the cupboard, pulled on their swimsuits and, clutching their towels, went dashing down the slope from the camp buildings to the sea. It was very close, only a hundred meters or so away.

On the beach, Olesya squinted in bliss. The southern sun took her in its embrace; the sea murmured its approval. She took a run and dived into the motionless salty water. The other girls followed her example. Polinka squealed with delight and Olya splashed about.

After breakfast Lidia gathered her charges for assembly. She surveyed the wet boys and girls, so pale by comparison with the previous shift.

Lidia didn't really like children. She had liked them at first, though. She had read journals that described various approaches to education. She knew how she ought to behave in any given situation. She knew a child wouldn't tell lies just for the sake of it, and that it was best not to try to stop them smoking, that, with the glamour of transgression removed, the problem would disappear all on its own. That children are people, just like grown-ups—they need understanding and respect. The books had taught her that children are courageous and kind, that any insolence and rudeness is just a reaction to the inappropriate behavior of adults.

Lidia had gone to teachers' training college. Then she'd gone to work in a nursery school. She'd seen her little wards—obstinate, withdrawn, tearful or lively. And she was going to teach them all to be kind and understanding. She loved children. Love could work miracles.

On the first day little Kolya Ezhikov had called her a "damn bitch." Lidia hadn't known how to react. She wanted to slap the poisonous sneer off that twisted little face. But physical violence would make her pedagogically and legally culpable.

"Go and wash your mouth out with soap!" she said in a hoarse voice.

"Cunt!" Kolya shouted cheerfully.

The matron came—a woman the size of a basketball player. She took Kolya by the scruff of his neck and led him off to the dormitory. Kolya had stayed there until lunch; then he'd threatened to complain to his father, who would "get all of you." They let him out.

Kolya wasn't the only surprise. Alyona Griman brought a rubber dildo to the nursery school and the whole group had played with it in secret until Lidia spotted them and confiscated it. She'd blushed bright red. Alyona had thrown a tantrum, demanding it back, and Kolya had laughed himself into hysterics. Red-faced, sweaty and nervous, Lidia had set off to complain to Nadezhda Semyonovna, but behind her back she'd heard Pasha Zaitsev whisper:

"She's going off for a fuck!"

Lidia had swung round and smacked Pasha between the eyes with the rubber dildo.

She was immediately afraid. Afraid that Pasha's dad might be another who would "get all of you." But no one came for Lidia, although she trembled in fear for an entire week. The class began to do as it was told. And Lidia realized that strength meant authority over a collective of children too. She began ruling by reward and punishment and became the kind of crude educator that she despised in the past.

Then she started working at the camps. Lidia got herself hired by a company, put together a group and took them to the south. Originally she'd thought she would combine work with pleasure and have a bit of a vacation herself. But the children had made sure there was no chance of that. All her time and nervous energy were channeled into keeping order. The children smoked behind the chalets, went swimming without asking permission and bought beer that tasted of herrings.

Lidia was disgusted and frightened by the children. They were like dogs—what if they bit you when you gave them a kick? And a human being was bigger than a dog. Eventually Lidia had turned into a "commanding officer"; she allowed the children some freedom in exchange for obedience. She changed.

And now here was another group of them lined up in front of her. She already knew that these children were the same as all the others—insolent, rude, vulgar. But there would be a couple of snitches among them, probably girls, who would tag along after her and whisper: "Kozlov's smoking in the chalet . . . Popova drank Guseva's compote . . . Lavkin swears . . ." And that there would be hard cases, too, who had fathers like Kolya Ezhikov's.

Lidia tried to conceal her fear and dislike. After all, she wasn't paid to turn her nose up in disgust. And anyway, Lidia knew some of these boys and girls: Klara Petrova, the daughter of a school friend of hers; Taras Eremeev, Klara's classmate; Lyova Dynin, the grandson of one of her mother's friends; Stasik Galkin, who lived on her block; and Valerii

Setkin, whose sister Nastya Setkina went to that disastrous nursery school. Valerii used to pick her up every day.

Yury Faddeevich Setkin, Valerii and Nastya's father, was the deputy director of the factory that had offered the subsidized places at the camp. He was a broad, stocky man with heavy, flaking cheeks and big, round eyes. He looked as though he was always surprised or always trying to frighten people in advance. Nastya looked like him; she had the same round features and her cheeks sagged in the same way. Not pretty. With a small mouth and little eyes like watermelon seeds. But she was a good girl, she didn't use foul language, she didn't cry all the time, she slept during the quiet hour and she didn't tell everyone what a big shot her dad was. Lidia had been very pleased with her. But not Nadezhda Semyonovna. "What a horribly sluggish and lazy child," she used to say of Natalya. "If only she'd kick up a fuss or get into a fight." But Nastya never caused a scene and she had her own special way of fighting: she drew back her little white hand without saying a word, and then drove her little fist into her opponent's nose. In that way she won the respect of the children, and Kolya Ezhikov trailed around after her like a dog, batting his pale eyelashes.

Valerii and his mother would pick up Natalya in a Volvo. Sweet-scented mom stayed in the car, snuggling down into her collar, while Valerii went to get Nastya and sign the register. Nastya hopped and skipped as she ran to meet her brother; it was the only time she ever showed any signs of animation. Valerii took her by the hand and led her off in silence.

The Setkins could have hired a nanny, but Nastya's mom was categorically opposed to the idea.

"If she's educated at home the girl will grow up unprepared for the world," she said. "A group, she must be in a group. Of little kids like herself."

Nastya's mom was desperately afraid her daughter would never learn to mix with other people.

Lidia cast an eye over the motley assembly and said:

"We assemble in an organized manner for breakfast, lunch, tea and supper, ten minutes before the start of the meal. I have no other restrictions to impose on you. Smoking and drinking alcohol in the camp is forbidden. So is appearing in a drunken state. Discipline is not an empty word. I hope you will all behave like decent human beings and not like escaped convicts. You must take care of your own clothes and keep yourselves clean. Look, Valerochka's had a haircut, unlike some of the rest of you! You can see right off how neat and tidy he is!"

Lidia pointed to Setkin. The boys and girls began giggling, but Ignat said in a loud, vicious voice:

"He's not neat and tidy, he's just a pain in the ass . . ."

"Mitnikov!" Lidia cut him short.

"And Mitnikov's just a stupid, ugly monkey," Valerochka retorted in a clear voice.

"Setkin and Mitnikov are cleaning out the chalets and washing the floors today," said Lidia in a tone that brooked no objections. The factory children had no intention of objecting.

And with that, the assembly was brought to an end.

* * *

They lay in wait for Valerochka behind the dining hall, where there was a small paved area concealed by clumps of cherry-plum trees. In the south it gets dark early even in summer. So Valerochka came unstuck in a big way.

Taras punched him in the nose and his glasses cracked with a crunch. Valerochka staggered back a few steps to avoid falling down, but he fell anyway when Ignat hit him from behind with an empty wooden crate. Valerochka grabbed for his belt buckle, but he didn't get the chance to unfasten it—Curly punched him in the stomach, right in the solar plexus. Valerochka doubled over, covering his face. They kicked him, swinging hard so that every blow shook his entire body.

Then Taras hoisted Valerochka up by his jacket (he never took his jacket off, even when it was hot) and Ignat snarled into his broken, bleeding face:

"Now, you bald fucker, who's the monkey?"

"You are," Valerochka answered.

He didn't remember anything after that.

Polinka was cleaning her white pants with her toothbrush.

"Look, I sat in something! Chewing gum probably!" she complained mournfully as Olesya came in.

Irka lay on the top bunk, singing in her throaty voice:

"Don't speak, I know just what you're saying . . ."

"Hey girls, I've heard there's going to be a dance," Olya said from the lower bunk.

"So?"

"So, we'll be able to meet boys!"

"Yeah right . . . With your special dimensions!" Olesya

chuckled to herself. Irka stopped singing and began rummaging in her handbag:

"But we can meet them where we like anyway. On the beach, for example! Sugar, where are my cigarettes? Ah, here they are . . . And anyway, there's no one here worth bothering about. We need to take a break from boys as well! Don't mind if I smoke, do you girls? I can go out on the balcony if you like."

They allowed her to smoke in the room. Of course, thought Olesya. Irka can afford to play hard-to-get, she's pretty, probably left more boys behind in town than she can count . . . But the best thing that tub of lard Olya can hope for is a summer romance! Then for some reason she remembered Valerochka. The thought of his ugly face made Olesya feel annoyed. She snuggled down under the blanket and began thinking how beautiful and warm the sea was, how nice the girls were and how Lidia wasn't too bad either, although she pretended to be strict, how they'd had rissoles with gravy and watermelon for lunch, and how . . .

She fell asleep, contented.

The girls spread the rumor at breakfast: Valerochka had a broken nose, a gash in his head and black eye. No, two black eyes.

Olesya felt frightened. Who'd done that to him? They said it was locals.

"Lawless bandits!" Olya exclaimed with her mouth full.

"That's shitty!" commented Irka. "Even down here you can't get any peace."

Polinka was a delicate creature, who never left the room

without her makeup on (even to go to the beach), but she was the one who challenged the gossip:

"It wasn't the locals!"

"Why not?"

"I reckon it was Mitnikov. They called each other names at assembly, didn't they? Over racial prejudice."

"Over what?" asked Olya, raising her eyes from her plate.

Polinka didn't hear her and carried on:

"So now, girls, we'll be able to live in peace and quiet, and screw fucking Valerochka anyway."

It was amazing that pale-lilac, sweet-smelling Polinka could talk that way.

Olesya met Valerochka three days later on the beach. Everyone was at the dance, up by the dining hall, but she wanted to be alone, so she walked out through the wall and down toward the sea.

He was sitting on a bench, shrouded in purple darkness on every side. Olesya didn't recognize him at first, but then he called to her:

"Hi!"

"Hi . . ."

"Come and sit down," Valerochka said.

Olesya sat down beside him reluctantly. She couldn't tell what she was feeling. Annoyance? Dislike? Indifference? She was silent. Valerochka spoke first.

"I suppose you heard what happened to me?"

"Yes . . ."

"Only don't get any ideas; they didn't break any bones."

"Well, I don't really . . ."

"Give a damn?" he guessed. He wasn't offended. He gazed into the distance, staring at the sea through his cracked glasses. Olesya felt ashamed of her indifference. She asked:

"What did they do?"

"Cracked the cartilage in my nose," Valerochka answered calmly, without looking at her. "That was all. Nothing much else. Don't worry about it. Although you weren't worried anyway."

He spoke lightly, without reproach, perhaps even cheerfully.

Someone ran down onto the beach, rustling the sand. They heard Irka's voice:

"Les! Are you there?"

"Yes!" Olesya responded. "I'll be going then?"

"Off you go," said Valerochka.

"Who was that you were talking to?" Irka asked as they walked along.

"Um, no one," Olesya said rather uncertainly. "Just one of the . . ."

Irka didn't let her finish.

"We've hooked up with Mitnikov, Taras and that . . ."

"Curly," Olesya prompted her.

"We're all going drinking!" Irka informed her happily, putting her arm round Olesya's shoulder. "We're going to have a genuine vacation! Don't mind if I smoke, do you?"

* * *

Ignat was surprised to see Olesya. Maybe he'd been hoping the "fourth girl" would be okay and Olya could be attached to Stasik, who was still hanging around. But that wasn't what Olya had in mind—she had her sights set on Taras. She'd put on pearly purple lipstick and eyeliner. She kept laughing, clucking like a mad chicken, but Taras was frowning. Ignat and Curly sighed in secret relief at their close call.

"Hi," Olesya tossed out brightly, noting Ignat's surprise. She felt a claw of annoyance scrape at her insides. What did you expect? she asked herself ruthlessly. You're not Irka, who looks so good even without makeup—green eyes, even if they are a bit small, plump lips with a dimple, long ginger curls down over her ears, a slim figure with taut, lean muscles under skin that's already tanned, and not Polinka—a delicate white-faced creature with a doll's mouth and carefully made up little eyes—a little tease with perfectly layered hair . . .

Ignat's ears suddenly blazed bright red. He'd noticed her glance and for some reason it had made him feel uncomfortable. I never promised her anything, he thought. All we did was tell each other our names. No one said anything about liking each other. But it would be a low trick to pretend we never said "hello" or smiled at each other now. Moron, he said to himself, she's not about to rape you.

Polinka was giggling merrily. Curly watched her tenderly, stroking her curls. Irka was smoking and studiously ignoring Taras—tall, wide-shouldered Taras with his bulging muscles, like a juvenile delinquent. Olesya had seen boys like that on television.

"Are we going then?" Ignat asked without looking at the girls.

The outdoor café smelled of fried onions and kebabs. A comfortable kind of smell. A fat woman with black hair and a mustache was leaning with her breasts propped up on the wooden counter that was scrubbed a clean yellow. A Georgian-looking man with his left arm in plaster was sitting beside her in long underwear, smoking. A boy was perched in readiness on a plastic chair with his brown legs pulled up under him. Every now and then he jumped down and ran over to the customers, holding a towel covered with stains over his pointed elbow.

The boy was dirty, with black hair, chapped lips and big black eyes. A good-looking boy. About twelve years old.

He came flying up to their group as they were awkwardly taking their seats at the long wooden table under a chestnut tree twined around with convolvulus.

"What would you like?"

Ignat was flustered, but Taras and Curly beamed happily and looked at the boy the same way they looked at everyone, and the goodwill that hovered over them infected everyone nearby. They had never gotten into discussions about just how much they meant to each other, never sworn brotherhood, or sworn they'd help each other if ever they were in trouble. They were friends who never argued, always delighting in the single fact that there was such a person as Taras Eremeev in the world, or such a person as Curly.

"We'll have kebabs and beer," Taras said.

Olya shivered, excited.

They gnawed on their kebabs in silence. Feeling shy. Irka smoked; she was above such childish awkwardness. Olya drank her beer in large gulps and Curly laughed and joked with her. He was prepared to share his happiness with anyone. Even fat Olya. Polinka picked at her meat like a bird, feeling grateful for Curly's magnanimity. Ignat shrugged off his lethargy, and started telling the others in a loud, cheerful voice how he went to the swimming pool and all about his dog Vulcan. Irka listened. Taras explained to Olesya what made Counter-Strike better than Ultima.

Olesya got up to pee.

"Amir, show her the way," yelled the woman with the mustache.

The black-eyed boy leapt down off his chair. He showed Olesya to a kind of outhouse and pointed to a door with a picture of a toadstool drawn on it.

Olesya rubbed her temples in the quiet of the stall. After the beer she'd drunk her head felt like it was a ball dangling on a string. She pulled the cord and there was a loud cascade of water. The bolt on the door clanked.

Back at the table, the feasting was at its height. Curly was dipping his meat into ketchup and smearing it all over his lips as he ate. Polinka was draped limply over her chair like a set of discarded clothes. Irka, Olya and Taras were gaping drunkenly at Ignat as he waved his arms about and sang:

> *I don't want your miserable handouts,*
> *I'll screw you anytime and anywhere.*
> *I know the only thing you need to know*
> *Is when you need it someone will be there.*
> *So if you want that someone to be tough,*
> *Then take a look my way and take me on.*
> *Quit moaning about jerks, I've had enough.*
> *I don't have time to flatten every one.*
> *You want your girlfriends sick with jealousy,*
> *Is that really what you want me to do?*
> *What stupid fucking good is that to me?*
> *Go fuck yourself, you bitch, fuck you.*

His ears were flushed a deep ruby red.

Lidia didn't even bother to reprimand them when she spotted them drunk at the gate. What a surprise . . . she thought in annoyance. At least Taras Eremeev, who was clutching Irka provocatively, stopped and turned his bleary eyes away. What's he doing squeezing her like that? Lidia wondered. She noticed Irka wasn't pressing back against Taras.

Curly was dragging Polinka along, who was curved over like a Turkish sword, and trying to tell her something, but she was giggling, not listening. Olesya and Ignat were walking along with their arms around each other. Ignat was bawling:

"I'll fuck over any ugly cunt. Just tell me, Olesya, if anybody tries anything . . . you let me know!"

Olesya smiled and agreed: she'd tell him, all right.

Plodding along behind the rest came Olya Kliueva, miserable as a poisoned elephant.

Lidia locked herself in her room and kicked off her flip-flops. She gave a deep sigh to eliminate all the negative energy of the day and counted: one, two three . . . The only thoughts left in her head were the warm sea, the hot white sand made of crushed shells, the cold plums from the market . . . her reverie didn't last.

No, Lidia thought as she lay down on the bed. This business with Setkin's not that simple . . . It must have been one of ours . . . maybe Mitnikov? Or perhaps it really was locals? They say there are whole gangs of them here . . . But what were they after? Money? She remembered the hard face of

the camp warden—tall, skinny Galina. "What does this boy
say? Nothing? Good, let him keep his mouth shut," she said
as she closed the door. "Your Setkin's bruises will heal up
soon enough, and the police would only stir up bad feeling
and spoil everybody's vacation. There's no point in bringing
in outsiders. If he's keeping his mouth shut, you do the
same." Lidia realized that she could keep quiet all right, but
Setkin would still tell the whole story to dear old dad, and
then her life wouldn't be worth living. Lidia pictured those
flabby cheeks with the razor burn, the intense stare of those
round eyes and the voice: "I see . . ." Lidia couldn't think of
anything to follow "I see," she simply couldn't imagine what
kind of vituperation Yury Faddeevich would rain down on
her head. And would it stop at just words? "Oh, help . . ."
Lidia squealed, and red blotches spread on her pasty white
face.

I've got to have a word with Mitnikov. Get him to apolo-
gize. But what if it's not Mitnikov? Tell Valerii not to tell his
dad? No, that's crazy . . .

From Setkin, Lidia's thoughts moved on to the others.

And now those idiots . . . Drunk . . . It all begins with
giggles and hugs, and then they'll end up happily giving
away their virginity! And who'll get the blame? She got a
cold, empty feeling in the pit of her stomach. And she remembered Kolya Ezhikov's little face twisted in fury: "Cunt!"

Someone scraped against the door of the balcony. Polinka
asked in a thin voice:

"Who's that, girls?"

"Who's there? Yogi Bear," Irka quipped, slurring her

words as she lay in bed holding a cigarette. Her fingers lost their grip and the cigarette fell on Polinka.

Olya snorted into her pillow and turned her face to the wall. Olesya leaned down from the top bunk and fumbled at the door with her nails. Her head felt like it was stuffed with cotton wool. She stuck her nose back into her pillow, feeling she couldn't move anymore.

Taras crept into the room, followed by Ignat and Curly. They were purposeful, as if they'd agreed on a plan in advance. Taras immediately reached up and clambered onto Irka's top bed, breathing out sweet alcohol fumes. She giggled throatily. Curly sat on the edge of Polinka's bed.

"Hi there," Polinka squeaked in a thin voice, lying there like a rag doll.

Olesya felt a vague aching in her belly and a frighteningly pleasant thought crept through the fog in her head: What's Ignat up to? He can't be here for Olya . . .

Taras found Irka's lips with his own and licked them with his hot tongue, breathing passionately. Irka responded. Then with one hand he started pulling off his track pants. His prick sprang out, hard and erect. Irka put her arms gently around his back. She snorted when Taras stuck his hand into her panties. He pulled them off, getting them tangled up on Irka's legs. He growled or laughed—it wasn't clear which. In a hurry, afraid that Irka would change her mind, he pushed her slim legs apart and directed his prick with his hand, thrust blindly for a moment, and then found the spot. With a suppressed squeal he pressed Irka's shoulders back against the bunched-up pillow.

Ignat watched with an imbecilic look on his face as Taras rocked sharply backward and forward with his gold chain dangling. He looked at Irka, who had spread her naked legs wide and turned her face away from Taras. He could see her big ginger curls on the pillow. Curly half stood up, staring wildly as he listened avidly to Taras's squealing and heavy breathing. In-out, in-out . . . Olesya couldn't figure out if the whole thing was a dream or not. And what if it wasn't? What if . . . What if . . . And why was Ignat standing there rooted to the ground like that? Why was it all happening?

Curly uttered a strange sound, grabbed hold of his pants between his legs and made a dash for the door and out onto the balcony. Olesya heard the hollow sound of his sneakers slapping against the ground.

Ignat slipped out after him.

Setkin didn't wear his jacket anymore; he dressed the same way as everyone else. He went around in a sleeveless T-shirt and shorts. But under his shorts he still wore his belt. The sun tanned his arms and legs and turned his shaved head pink. His cracked glasses were the only reminder left of what Lidia's boss had said: "The police will only stir up bad feeling and spoil everyone's vacation . . ."

Lidia tried to talk to him. The important thing is not to lose his respect! she thought feverishly. With that in mind she approached Valerochka after lunch.

"Setkin! What's been going on?" Her voice was strange, unnatural. Valerochka twitched his nose and glanced indifferently at Lidia. "I'm talking to you. Your mother's . . . bound to find out! Your father too . . ." Lidia faltered. "What will he do to you?"

Valerochka pulled on his nose and narrowed his eyes

mockingly. Then he walked carefully and deliberately around Lidia and set off toward the dormitory blocks. Lidia tried to stop the trembling in her legs. "Cocky bastard," she whispered to herself.

Unlike Lidia, Valerochka wasn't too concerned about the fact that his head had been beaten in. That unlovely face radiated a wholesome serenity.

He was still wearing that expression when he turned the corner from behind one of the blocks and came across four boys and little Stasik, jumping about like a puppy.

"Beat it, shithead!" the boys shouted to Valerochka, tossing a pair of swimming goggles back and forth.

"Give him one, Dynin!"

"What's that asshole doing here? Let's work the fucker over, guys!"

"Fuck off, freak!"

Valerochka knitted his dark eyebrows in puzzlement, but he didn't slow his stride. He walked straight up to the group, his hand reaching for his shorts. The four watched cautiously and even stopped swearing. They were wondering if maybe baldy four-eyes had come to make peace. They're going to pulverize me; I'm fucked . . . Valerochka thought. Better not interfere. He would have walked on by, but Stasik grabbed hold of his shorts despairingly.

"They took my goggles!"

That's it! The little bastard's gotten me into it . . . Valerochka's heart sank.

"Give the goggles back. Pronto."

The foursome looked at him, sizing him up, wondering if they could take him on. Then one after another they started smiling: sure they could.

"Suck our cocks, asshole."

"You'll pay for that," Valerochka replied calmly, trying to hold his quivering nerves in check.

"Go fuck yourself!" said the biggest of the guys, a little taller than Valerochka.

He got it first. The buckle whistled through the air and bit into his cheek. The guy squealed. The other three dashed at Valerochka. One, skinny, with tangled hair and a Metallica T-shirt, got to Valerochka first and stars exploded in front of his right eye as his fist made contact. Fuck them, fuck the shitty bastards—the words went round and round in Valerochka's head. Without bothering to defend himself, he lashed left and right with his buckle, almost always hitting the target. Without even feeling their punches, he worked away intently with his fists, aiming to hit them in the throat. But one of them got in a kick just below Valerochka's knee and his leg folded under him, leaving him half sitting. Immediately they knocked him to the ground with a blow to the chest. And then they went at it. Choking on blood and snot, the one with the slashed cheek jumped in the air and landed with his feet on Valerochka's head.

Why the fuck did I interfere? Valerochka wondered, with tears in his eyes. Stasik was wailing. He didn't want his goggles anymore; he just wanted them to stop. Maybe I ought to remember the faces, thought Valerochka.

"One of yours again!" the warden said, turning crimson. "The same one again!"

"Setkin . . ."

"Don't you even bother to keep an eye on them? Do

they just wander about . . . free as the wind?" The commandant waved her arm in the air as she spoke.

"What's that got to do with it?" Lidia snarled back, sens-
ing the approach of inevitable doom: "I see . . ."

"There's no discipline at all in your group! If the police
take an interest in these incidents, it'll be a stain on the
camp's name!"

"And so," said the warden, wiping the sweat off her neck,
"you must do something about it, Lidia Mikhailovna. Can't
his parents come and collect him? No, of course, that's no
good . . . His bruises will have healed before the group
leaves anyway . . . And if we call in the parents now they'll
make one hell of a fuss! Do you understand what I want?"

"No, I don't," Lidia confessed in a cool tone of voice.
"What do you suggest we do with Setkin?"

"You can keep him by your side at all times," said the
commandant, smacking her lips triumphantly.

"What idiotic kind of idea is that? That's ridiculous!"
Lidia said. She trudged wearily out of the cool office into the
heat.

Setkin was waiting by the building, holding his swollen
cheek. He glanced at Lidia indifferently. She was used to
children looking at her that way. She tried to curry favor
with them so that they wouldn't isolate her, so she wouldn't
find herself in a situation where the words "fucking bitch"
left her powerless to do anything. But she didn't know how
to behave like them, so it was better to make herself seem remote, unapproachable.

"Okay?" Valerochka asked feebly. "Can I go now?"

"Just exactly what is the problem here?" asked Lidia,
pursing her lips. "Why are you always getting beaten up?"

Valerochka shrugged his tanned shoulders irritably. Lidia

saw a belt buckle sticking out from under his T-shirt, with an army star and the letters "V.S." in the corner.

"Can I go now?" Valerochka repeated.

"Yes."

He stuck his hands into the pockets of his shorts, walked past Lidia and off in the direction of the sea.

On the beach he got undressed and lay down on the crushed shells. He put his T-shirt on his face, plunging himself into stuffy darkness. The sun enveloped him in its rays. There were little kids running around. He could hear splashing water and bursts of laughter.

Fuck it, Valerochka thought gloomily. There's so many of them against me now . . . those three . . . plus that other four . . . seven . . . that's a few too many . . .

Not far away, Klara Petrova was sunbathing beside a boatman's hut. Her two thick braids lay at her sides as though they were sunbathing separately, independently of her. The ring in her nose glittered, reflected in Taras's eyes as he stood over her.

"Klara," he growled uncertainly, "they say you're going to transfer to the lycée in tenth class."

"Leave me alone," said Klara, frowning without even opening her eyes.

"Just like that, 'leave me alone'?"

Klara twitched her nose like a hamster and maintained a tense silence.

"Let's go for a walk this evening," Taras suggested.

"Eremeev," said Klara, opening her eyes and trying to assume a fierce expression, "you're disturbing my rest!"

"Why, am I in your sun, or what?" Taras exclaimed angrily. Klara softened.

"Okay . . ."

From a distance Irka watched Taras's happy face and Klara's indifference, feeling as if she was eating hot sand by the handful. Her throat burned.

Polinka and Olesya maintained a tactful silence. Both were confused, uncertain about their own feelings. Should they be delighted nothing "like that" had happened to them, or afraid—"What if?" Perhaps they should be sorry for Irka and angry with Taras, Ignat and Curly . . .

Olya was quietly triumphant. Her failure to ensnare Taras had suddenly been transformed into prudence—of course, she'd known in advance nothing good could be expected from those morons, nothing but trouble.

Irka leapt to her feet and walked away, raking her feet through the shells. The other girls watched her go. Irka's shoulders jerked, as though she could feel their eyes on her. She stumbled, kicking up a spray of sand.

"Watch where the fuck you're going," Valerochka growled angrily from under his T-shirt. He lifted it up. Irka saw the black eye and the cheekbone gashed by the same blow, the scratches on the lips and shaved head.

"What?" muttered Valerochka. "Fuck off, go on . . ."

He pulled the T-shirt back over his head.

Taras pressed himself against Klara, but she pursed her lips and moved away. Taras tried it again and again, and she pushed him away. The music was blaring loudly, the colored lights were blinking. Klara danced, her short skirt swirling around her hips. Ignat and Curly were guffawing nearby— they'd managed to get down to the kiosk for some beer after supper. They forced their way into the circles of dancers, laughing and grabbing at the girls' hands, and the girls giggled as they fought them off.

Those two "meatheads," as Klara Petrova referred to them, were also in a high mood because half an hour earlier they'd written "fuck da Setkin" in whitewash on the wall of block four, which stood sideways to the beach, where everyone could see it. They'd written it big, made a real effort. And now they were feeling good.

Curly, Ignat and Taras had acquired a firm reputation as hard cases. Boys were afraid of them. And all the girls wanted them to be their boyfriends. Katya Moiseeva, fourteen years old, with her carefully applied lipstick and straight black hair, was in no hurry to pull the sleeve of her see-through blouse out of Ignat's sweaty hands. She was dancing really close to him. "Where are those hands of yours, where are your hands, let's all lift up our hands and dance!" Katya Moiseeva lifted up her hands and dropped them onto Ignat's shoulders. Without even pausing to think he leaned toward her mouth and smudged her lipstick. Katya sucked in his saliva.

They moved away from the dancing boys and girls and the little kids who were whirling about. Staggering drunkenly, they went behind the dining hall, to the little paved square surrounded by clumps of cherry plum. They put their arms around each other. Not too rough, though, or she'll run for it . . . Ignat thought automatically. His hands slithered over Katya's trembling hips. Ignat suddenly felt afraid and excited all at once. As he pressed her closer he felt a sinking sensation in his heart and a strange tingling in his belly. Out of the corner of his eye he noticed the wide stone barrier of the square, overgrown with some low weed that looked like moss. He led Katya over to it and pulled her down. Katya lay down obediently and her hands began sweating with the excitement . . . Hastily, too hastily, Ignat began pulling down Moiseeva's panties, but she didn't object. She even pulled Ignat's trousers down herself. Ignat slumped on top of her and fumbled about, setting his prick to her with his hands. He swayed forward sharply. Katya was breathing heavily in fright. His prick skidded across her hips. Ignat hissed in a barely audible whisper: "Agh, bitch . . ." He pushed her legs further apart. Using both hands, he finally managed to stick his prick into her. Katya gasped, crushed under Ignat's weight. He began thrashing about feverishly, propping himself up on his hands and two minutes later his sweaty face dropped against Katya's shoulder. She was frightened by his drooping, wet lips, his open mouth and empty eyes. She jerked about frantically, but he just swayed a bit and kept lying there with his legs dangling. Katya almost burst into tears. Panicking, she scratched at Ignat with her fingers as she tried to squirm out from under him. She sobbed:

"Shit, what the hell's up with you?"

Ignat shook his tow-haired head and started to come around.

"What's up with me, bunny? I love you! Love you . . . Ever since we arrived . . . Bunny . . ."

He couldn't remember her name.

"Honest?"

"Honest, bunny."

Katya was swamped by a wave of warm feeling. So this is love, she thought happily, reassuring herself.

"I love you too, Ignat."

* * *

Valerochka sat on the balustrade of the balcony with his legs
on the outside, writing on the back of a cream-soda label:

1. Mitnikov—block 6
2. Eremeev—block 6
3. Curly—block 6
4. Dynin—block 4
5. Puzaty—block 4
6. Gena Zh.—block 4
7. Artyom—block 4.

Stasik, who had obligingly provided the information, was
beside him. Gazing into Valerochka's eyes.

"And every evening Ignat, Curly and Taras go to a café!
It's called The Chairs!"

"You mean The Twelve Chairs?"

"Yes! Right after supper," Stasik announced, curling up
his lips into a smile.

"Thanks," Valerochka said coolly, jumping down off the
balustrade onto the balcony and disappearing into his room.
Stasik picked at a scratch on his nose and ran off to the beach.

Valerochka lay on the top bunk bed in his room, holding
the label up in front of his eyes and moving his lips sound-
lessly. Am I going to spend my entire vacation putting this
bunch in order? I could finish off these bastards in one
week . . . but fuck, they never go anywhere alone . . . Except
to piss at the café . . . But that's just total lunacy—ambush-
ing them outside the restroom . . . Fuck . . . His thoughts
trailed away to nothing.

* * *

"I screwed that one," Ignat boasted, pointing through the glass at Katya Moiseeva.

"Class," said Curly with an envious laugh as he pulled off a T-shirt spattered with white paint.

Taras nodded his head in approval, with the wise expression of a man of the world.

"What's she doing sitting out there?" asked Curly.

Ignat shrugged.

Katya Moiseeva was sitting on the bench outside block 6, looking up at the boys' balcony and the door of the building. She was wearing that same transparent synthetic blouse. She began sweating. She squirmed impatiently, stirring up the sand with her foot.

"She'll stick to you like glue now," Taras said.

Ignat frowned.

"A real whore," Curly commented uncertainly after a moment's thought.

"Did she suck you off?" Taras inquired in a serious voice.

"Yes, I mean no," said Ignat. "Nah, she didn't suck me off."

Katya looked over the windows of the block and settled herself more comfortably on the bench. She clearly intended to sit there until Ignat came out.

"So what are you going to do?" asked Taras, screwing up his eyes mockingly.

"I don't know . . ."

Ignat was angry. He didn't want Katya running after him, thinking he loved her. He couldn't have her hanging around his neck, not even for the sake of a second go. The idea was repulsive. That's sex for you, he thought. Shit . . .

"What about Klara?" he asked, suddenly remembering.

"What about her?" said Taras, with a frown. He would

have liked to boast, but instead he blurted out the truth. "She told me to fuck off . . . Just like that . . . So I went. Didn't even try to kiss her . . ."

"Hmm," Curly mooed in sympathy. "Okay, let's go . . ." They went out into the hall and jumped down outside from the little boys' balcony. Katya was left waiting.

Irka lay on the beach, with Polinka, Olesya and Olya eating grapes beside her. They weren't talking about boys. Irka had dug up some crabs from under the sand and now Olya was turning them over and over with a stick.

Olesya squinted sideways at an older boy in blue shorts: half of his face was swathed in bandages. Oh yea-ah . . . she thought to herself. Fantômas. Has everyone around here gone crazy or what?

The boy was sitting on the sand, strumming a guitar and singing:

"Changes! We're waiting for changes!"

There were other boys, a bit smaller, lying sprawled around him. They were drinking fizzy drinks and listening, relaxing. One of them, the smallest but not the youngest, winked at Olesya. She blushed.

He crawled over to them, lizard-like, with an idiotic smile on his face. He looked the girls over and said cheerfully:

"My name's Gena!"

"Ah, like the crocodile in the cartoon," Irka replied indifferently, putting her cigarette out in the sand.

"Crocodile yourself," said Gena, offended.

Polinka laughed. Her laughter helped Gena forget Irka's rudeness.

"Hey, what's that you've got there?" he exclaimed, pointing at the crabs. He was as excited as a child. His cracked lips spread into a wide smile.

"Crabs!" Olya replied pompously, trying to look as if she wasn't afraid of crabs at all.

"Hey, guys!" Gena shouted in the direction of the boy with the guitar. "There's crabs over here!"

The boys stirred on the sand, got up and came over. Every single one of them had a bored expression on his face. Gena was the only one who smiled openly, shaking his raven-black bangs. He began the introductions.

"This is Tema, this is Puzaty and this is Dynin!"

"What happened to Dynin's face?" Irka asked.

"I fell and hit it on a bench," said Dynin reluctantly.

"Well I never," said Irka with a faint smirk. "Suddenly everybody's hitting themselves on benches . . ."

Gena turned his head this way and that like a raven.

Lidia's head throbbed. She lay there on the bed, gazing blankly up at the ceiling. She sat up, and took hold of a folder containing neatly arranged birth certificates and money. "Kriukova, Irina Alexandrovna . . ." Lidia remembered that yesterday she'd come and asked for a hundred rubles. Then she'd sat there on the bed with her neck twisted around oddly. Lidia had wanted to ask her what was wrong, but she'd felt embarrassed. It was awkward. "Mitnikov, Ignat Sergeevich . . ." Lidia had no doubt he was the one who'd daubed those words on the wall. The warden had almost choked on her fury. No one walking up from the beach could possibly miss those white letters on the dark-blue background.

Lidia reached for a bottle of mineral water. The folder tipped over and the documents slid out onto the floor with a gentle rustling sound. "Damn . . ." she bent over and gathered them up.

"Setkin, Valerii Yurievich . . ." Why the hell had Yury Faddeevich sent his son and heir to the camp when he could just as easily have sent him to Switzerland? Ah, but of course. He had to grow up in a group of "kids like himself." Learn to socialize. To get along with people. He couldn't have suspected his son would be subjected to systematic beatings here as a result of his group leader's negligence.

Lidia felt a sudden chill. She closed the folder and lay down on the bed. Oh God! Oh God!

Little Kolya Ezhikov surfaced cheerfully again: "Cunt!"

Most days now Valerochka went out of the camp into the town and walked along the narrow, quiet streets overhung with grapevines and walnut trees. During the day there was almost no one around; just occasionally he came across little boys in wet trunks and little girls carrying shopping bags with onions poking out of them. Valerochka walked along with his hands stuck in the pockets of his shorts. He looked at the houses, imposing, like castles. He peered into the dark amusement arcades, with their piles of old televisions and battered plastic Sony PlayStations.

He turned into a narrow side street overgrown with chestnut trees. He kicked the prickly little spheres as he walked along. The wind blew in under his T-shirt: Bastards . . . he thought calmly . . . "fuck da Setkin" . . . the shitty freaks . . . He lifted his eyes from the ground.

Two figures came toward him. One older and one younger. The older one had a shaved head and was wearing a T-shirt with the sleeves cut off. He twirled a chain in his hands. The younger one, about the same age as Valerochka, also had a shaved head and walked with his fists stuck in the pockets of his khaki shorts. Valerochka broke his stride, glancing into both of their faces in turn, then looked away, because the older one gave him a glance from under his bushy eyebrows. Zing-zing, went the chain. Valerochka walked past them and then stopped. He turned around slowly.

They were standing still, watching him . . .

Polinka had fallen in love. She told the others herself.

"I've fallen in love." Then she added happily: "With the crocodile!"

"You're a fool then!" Irka retorted, mimicking her voice.

They all laughed. Olesya was sitting on the floor cross-legged, drinking Cahors out of a plastic cup in small sips. They'd been drinking Cahors all day. Walking around with blue teeth. Laughing. With Irka singing in English: *"Don't speak, I know just what you're saying!"* and *"Gotta puke!"* to the tune of "Only You." It was three o'clock in the morning. They roared with laughter in the darkness, and their neighbors hammered on the walls, sparking new fits of laughter.

The girls settled into a routine, getting up at half past seven, feeling like dead fish, and slouching off to breakfast. Then they slept until lunchtime, ate lunch and went swimming and sunbathing until dinnertime. After dinner they went with Puzaty, Gena, Tema and Dynin into town to drink beer. There was no hassle with these boys. Nobody tried to get into the girls' panties. They wandered around, talking about everything under the sun. And even Olya had someone to keep her company—skinny, long-haired Tema in his Metallica T-shirt . . .

But for once, this evening they hadn't gone anywhere. They sat in the girls' room eating watermelon. The juice dribbled onto the floor and the seeds floated in it like black cockroaches. Irka crooned in her throaty voice: *"Gotta puke . . . Each day I puke a bit . . . La-la-la . . . la-la . . ."*

The others laughed till they choked. Then Gena noticed there was no beer left, so they decided to go for some more. Irka, Olya, and Polinka ran to join the line for the bathroom. Olesya was alone. After the laughter a strange silence descended. She giggled. She heard a light tap. A little white celluloid ball bounced across the floor from the window. Olesya stared in fright. The window was firmly closed. She caught the little ball—for a brief second its cold surface seared her fingers; then it warmed up in her grasp. She shook herself and thought, One of the girls must have put it on the windowsill.

The warden burst into Lidia's room at one in the morning.

"Lidia Mikhailovna! I warned you! I warned you!"

She kept repeating the words over and over again, with more emphasis every time. The first thought that flashed through Lidia's head was: Setkin's dead. And then, a fast forward: that vitriolic "I see . . .", the courtroom, the punches to the face and the kidneys, and fear, fear, fear.

Lidia ran to the telephone. Through the crackling she could just make out a dull voice that introduced itself and asked who she was. "Ah, the group leader? Excellent . . . then you should come immediately." She wrote down the address, struggling to control her fingers. Then she grabbed the warden by the arm. Together they ran to the gates of the camp.

The local policeman had exaggerated the scale of the incident. Whether deliberately or not, Lidia didn't know. She ran through the damp, echoing halls of the emergency room with the warden galloping along beside her. Catching glimpses of bandages and green blotches of ointment.

Curly had suffered the worst damage; he'd lost teeth—his front ones. And he had bruises all over his body and a black eye. They'd stitched up the gash on Taras's head. Ignat had gotten away with a broken nose and swollen wrist. Broken or sprained? Lidia feverishly tried to guess. Gena the crocodile was clutching his battered face: both of his eyes had been reduced to purple slits. Tema was howling as a nurse bandaged his fingers. Looking at his grimace of pain and blood-soaked Metallica shirt, Lidia had to bite her lip in order not to start howling herself. Just what is all this? Damn the whole lot of them, and all their broken noses and hands! To hell with them all!

Leva Dynin sat on a low chair, looking up at Lidia with resignation. His head looked like a cocoon now, because the cheekbone that was already bandaged had been joined by a torn ear and two new wounds on the top of his head. Puzaty sat there absolutely still while a doctor put his dislocated nose back in joint.

"Where's our beer then?" Polinka whined tearfully.

"They must have all dropped dead or something," said Irka, abandoning her cigarette. "Okay, let's go to bed!"

* * *

Lidia sat down on a chair covered in gray paint and caught her breath. They asked her to wait, and she tried to be patient, but the indignation was bursting out of her, demanding movement, a chance at least to release the tension somehow.

The policeman sat down beside her.

"Who did this to them?" Lidia gasped. She could barely control her tongue.

"According to their testimony they were youths, about ten of them . . . They beat them with chains and sticks . . . and kicked them."

"One at a time?"

"Four of them were picked up near the phone booths on Morozov Street. Then half an hour later there was a second incident—near the Twelve Chairs café. It's only a twenty-minute walk from the phone booths down to the Chairs. Ten or fifteen minutes if you run. It was the same gang that did it." The policeman wiped the sweat off his face. "Bastards . . ."

"Youths—what age exactly?" asked Lidia.

"Fourteen to eighteen," the policeman replied, breathing heavily as he dabbed at his red face with the handkerchief. "They don't even let you get any sleep, going after the kids from the camp. Scumbags."

"Will they be caught?" Lidia asked.

The policeman gestured hopelessly.

"I don't think so. There aren't any witnesses . . . not . . . a . . . thing," he said in the same tone in which he'd told her to come "imm-ed-iate-ly."

Lidia sat in silence, trying desperately to think. The policeman suddenly started and asked:

"Does this belong to one of your seven?"

Lidia glanced down and choked on her breath.

The policeman was holding a belt buckle. With an army star and the letters "V.S." in the corner.

"I found it near the café," the policeman explained.

"No . . . it, it's not ours . . . no," Lidia said, trembling.

The policeman laid an awkward hand on her shoulder.

"Don't upset yourself like that . . . The bruises will heal soon enough . . . It'll all blow over."

There were two weeks of camp remaining.

The bruises will heal, Lidia thought to herself. And it's a good thing they were beaten by strangers, not ours. What could I have done? She lay there, watching the hazy approach of dawn through the closet mirror. Consoling herself, persuading herself it would be all right. Forbidding herself to think about the consequences, about the parents. Anybody could shoot his mouth off if he had someone to hide behind. Mitnikov hid behind Taras and Curly. Dynin hid behind his trio . . . Kolya Ezhikov hid behind his dad . . . But whom did she have to hide behind?

Suddenly she jerked up off the bed.

But at least Setkin won't say anything to his dad, not . . . a . . . word! she thought, emphasizing the syllables like the policeman had. Because then it would come out that he beat up his own campmates . . . although . . . his father is the deputy director . . . And the parents of all the others work under him . . . Setkin's out of reach . . . Not . . . a . . . thing will happen to him! Or will it? What about his mom, who'd burst a blood vessel to prevent him dropping out of the group? The group of campers, because a street gang isn't a group, it's a whirlpool that draws a child into using drugs and drink . . . I should just tell Setkin that I know everything. Lidia imagined how she would say it, calmly and firmly. And she imagined Setkin's fear.

Setkin wasn't frightened. He shrugged and wrinkled up his little forehead in a frown.

"What do you know?"

"That it was you who beat up Mitnikov." (For some reason Lidia singled out Ignat from all the others.)

"There's no proof," said Valerochka with a calm shake of his head. "It was an outside gang."

"Yes, there is proof," said Lidia. "They found your buckle. And if I tell them that it's yours, then . . ."

Valerochka still wasn't surprised or frightened. He smiled with his wet mouth and simply said:

"Don't tell them. It's not important . . ."

Lidia saw his eyes: friendly eyes with mischievous sparks in the iris. It unnerved her. Children didn't talk like that; they didn't look like that.

"Okay, I won't tell them," she muttered. And the expression that she installed so carefully on her face every morning changed from strict to soft and stupid.

The policeman was right, the bruises did heal. The boys left the camp fit and well, if you didn't count the scars and missing teeth. And Tema's fingers.

But that was no big problem, thought Lidia, with a sigh. The warden agreed with a little nod of her head.

Ignat, Taras, Curly, Dynin and the others laughed as if nothing at all had happened. They dragged their suitcases and bags off the train onto the platform. Katya Moiseeva wrote down Ignat's telephone number. "Two-three-one-four-one-eight . . ." Although it wasn't one-four, it was three-eight. But that was only a couple of digits. Taras chewed on a match, glancing at Klara and Irka. Stasik Galkin stood beside him with his suitcase, tense and red-faced.

Olesya turned her head this way and that. Suddenly in the crowd of noisy, happy faces she spotted the wet, crooked mouth with the raised upper lip and the rabbit's teeth. The glasses bound up with sticky tape. The wet, black crew cut sticking up on the small head.

Valerochka squeezed his way through to her and took hold of her hand without speaking.

"Oles . . ." he whispered, when they'd moved away from the crowd a bit. "Will you . . ."

"What?"

Olesya noticed that he was all spruced up: he'd put on a fresh sports shirt under his jacket and tried to smooth out his overgrown crew cut. She couldn't understand whether she liked this ugly tapeworm or detested him. She wanted to press her mouth against his half-open lips and at the same time smash them with a dirty chunk of wood.

He said nothing. Then he bit his lip cheerfully and said:

"Will you give me your phone number?"

"What for?"

"So I can call you." Valerochka wasn't surprised by the question. He was tannned, his shoulders had expanded; that constantly easy, cheerful expression on his face had been re-placed by a bloom of smug satisfaction.

A hard case, Olesya thought skeptically. She noticed that Ignat, Taras and Curly avoided the subject of "fuck da Setkin" when they were talking with all their Klaras and Katyas, although earlier they'd boasted about it. They'd come back battered and beaten, but quiet. Setkin had sat be-side them in the dining hall and they'd ignored him, didn't scare him off like before. It was incredible.

Polinka laughed a happy little laugh and hugged Gena the Crocodile. Promised to call and write. To meet up some-time. Definitely. Olya huffed and puffed beside her. Tema had given her the slip, deciding a summer romance should be kept within the limits of the genre. Beside Olya, Dynin and Puzaty were bouncing up and down, along with Klara Petrova. What did she want with those guys?

"Will you give me your number?" Valerochka asked again, adjusting the knapsack on his shoulder.

"Five-three-zero-three-one-zero," Olesya replied, looking at his cracked glasses. Behind them she could see the light gray eyes with the fine golden veins. Valerochka wrote the number on his palm. In big numbers, circling every digit.

What did it matter if it wasn't one-zero, but seven-six. It was only a couple of digits. So what.

Olesya tidied her bangs and pushed her glasses up tight on her nose. Valerochka saluted and walked back toward the crowd.

Lidia drew her "factory kids" up into columns for the last time, reminded them cheerfully not to forget their things and gave the loud order: March! The boys and girls set off to-ward the exit. Suntanned, rosy-cheeked, plump-faced.

"Mommy," Stasik Galkin called out happily.

a song for the lovers

But even so, better to die that way
Than never loving anyone
Dolphin

1

I was waiting for my sausage to cook. With the speakers
blaring: *You can't say I didn't give it, I won't wait another minute!*

Oleg called and said that if I didn't come right away,
he'd jump out of the window. It's not like he's one of my ad-
mirers or anything. Just someone I know. I told him:

"I'm eating."

"So what?" He was amazed. "A man's about to end his
life, and you're eating!"

"Ah, come on . . ."

He sent this judgmental silence through the phone and then said:

"You're acting like you couldn't give a shit about me."

I didn't see why it should be any other way. Then Oleg hung up.

Oleg's a musician. He plays guitar in a band he put together with guys in his year at university (which is my year too). They used to play the local clubs and after a gig they'd all get wasted and just lie around. Seryoga, the bass player, never used to dry out at all. He kept falling off the stage. He shaved his head and went around with it covered in fuzz. Anton, the drummer, was into piercing and grass. He got high and played music. And he was brilliant. If he hadn't been high all the time, he could have written music. But he liked getting high more. Oleg wrote the music. He lived in the student residence, but he didn't live there really, he bummed round his friends' places with Seryoga. Or hung out at Anton's place, smoking dope. One time they organized a party and invited the whole class. I went with Svetka, a girl-friend of mine. Afterward if anyone asked the band who Svetka Ryabova was, they looked delighted and pushed their cheeks out with their tongues. Although I couldn't see how they could have remembered anything. It must have been from what other people told them, because everybody there, with almost no exceptions, was out of it. Lyokha Petrov puked on the carpet, but Anton didn't give him a hard time. He was totally out of it too.

The air was so blue it stung your eyes. Nastya Kulakova was smoking nonstop. Oleg and this other guy, Sashka Berdy-

shev, were singing songs, some their own and some other people's. Galya Romanova and Seryoga were screwing in the
bathroom. I was slouching from one corner to another, looking for a place to sit down. Then I went into the kitchen.

Masha Nikonova and Kostya Patrushev were sitting on
the windowsill. Kostya was smoking and Masha was drinking
vodka from the bottle.

"Hi," Kostya said to me.

"Hi," I answered.

Masha gave us a pensive look and held out the bottle to
me with a sigh.

"Want some?"

She'd brought it in secretly and kept it hidden all evening
so it wouldn't get taken from her and drunk by everybody.

"No thanks," I answered, and Masha gave a shrug. She
couldn't figure out why anyone could not want to get wasted.

Kostya stubbed his cigarette out against the window and
went into the room. He wanted to kiss her, but all Masha
wanted was to get drunk. They were out of sync. And on top
of that Masha was chronically lovesick for an older student,
Steklov, so she didn't even notice that anyone else existed.

"How's that Steklov of yours?" I asked her. There was a
time when Masha couldn't talk about anyone except Steklov,
and I won her over by listening to her talk about him for
hours on end.

"Fine," Masha growled and took a swig from the bottle.

She was obviously burnt out. Dead batteries. She didn't
say anything, but she was thinking about him all the time. I
could feel it. I sat down beside her on the windowsill and we
sat there looking out at the black oily gleam of the asphalt
and the bright drops of the streetlights reflected in the puddles. Masha drank and said nothing.

There was a rumble and crash in the other room and then laughter. Oleg came into the kitchen, wet and red-faced. He sat down with us, lit up and explained cheerfully:

"Lyokha went to sleep on top of the wardrobe and tumbled off the fucker. And he smashed the table."

"Is he okay?" asked Masha.

"Dunno," he said with a shrug.

The three of us sat there for a while, then Masha went off to find a place to sleep. Oleg brought a guitar and started singing to me. Everybody was asleep, but we were sitting there on the windowsill, him singing. And smoking. He left the kitchen for a minute and came back with a teapot.

"You drink tea here then?" I asked.

"Did you think there was nothing but vodka?"

"Yep." I nodded.

We drank tea without talking. Suddenly he lifted his head like he'd just woken up and asked:

"Have you seen the new Richard Ashcroft video?"

"Where he's waiting for a girl and he doesn't hear her knocking, then he's waiting for her again? And then he goes to take a piss?"

"Nah . . . he doesn't go to take a piss. He thinks there's someone in the bathroom, so he goes in. The faucet's running."

"He's taking a piss."

"Nah! She's in there."

"So how did she get in?"

Oleg stuck out his lip and shrugged.

"She dropped by. She even made a meal."

"No way! The meal was already cooked, he made it, then he couldn't hold out any longer and he ate it. And he kept turning the music on and off."

"Okay then." Oleg pushed his face away. "Let's say there wasn't any girl and Richard Ashcroft went to take a piss." I nodded, and he went on. "But he switched off the music when he thought . . . when he went to take a piss according to your version. Right?"

"Right."

"So who turned the music on?"

"Maybe that was the girl?" I asked uncertainly.

"Aha!"

We said nothing for a while. Then Oleg said:

"It's called 'A Song for the Lovers.' That must be the way it always is for lovers. Will she come or won't she, will she turn it on or won't she? On MTV they translated it as 'Song for People in Love.' But it's about lovers. The translation's wrong."

"What's the difference?"

"People in love—that's a husband and wife. Just for the sake of a rough comparison. But lovers haven't got any legal rights . . ."

"Don't they owe each other anything?"

Oleg smiled and lit up. "People don't owe anybody anything anyway."

We were silent for a while. Oleg took a drag on his cigarette, squinting against the smoke. Then he stubbed it out in a saucer and picked up his guitar.

"Play something of your own," I asked him.

But he thought for a moment and started playing "A Song for the Lovers." He picked out the tune and sang, lost it and started picking it out again. And then we went off to sleep.

* * *

The sausage was boiled. I stuck it into the slit in a long bun and poured ketchup over it. Now I had a hot dog. The English term doesn't really mean a dog that's hot, it means "excited dog," because the sausage looks like a certain part of the dog's body . . . Or that's what the Americans thought. Lyokha Petrov told me that.

The phone rang again. I picked it up.

"Hello."

"Finished eating yet?"

"No."

After the party Oleg went missing, and when they had sobered up, Seryoga and Anton spent two days looking for him. On the third day they found him. Or rather, he turned up. He'd gone off to another town with some girl. He couldn't remember her name. Or maybe he could, but he wasn't saying.

Later the whole class went to a gig by Oleg and his band in some shitty club. Everyone got wasted again and wound up in heaps in corners. Masha sat on her own, sober and lost in thought. I sat down beside her with a can of gin.

"How's that Steklov of yours getting on?"

Masha brightened up and gave me a tormented smile:

"Fine . . ."

"And you?"

Masha didn't understand the question.

"Fine," she repeated, the way people talk when the bus driver asks "How are you paying?" for the second time.

I shrugged and took a swig from the can. Oleg came out onstage with his guitar. Some guy with a greasy face started applauding him like crazy. Oleg switched his guitar on and stood there on his own. Seryoga and Anton were lying in the restroom, out of it. Oleg was out of it too. He swayed forward and grabbed hold of the microphone. There was this earsplitting screech. Oleg shook his head and started playing. And singing.

Masha listened with her cheek propped on her palm. Every song she heard was about Steklov. So she liked all kinds of music.

Oleg sang and everyone else drank or just lay around on the floor and on the tables. That must be annoying. When all you can see is a roomful of drunks. When you're singing and no one hears you. And not even because they're not listening. I got up and went over to the stage. Oleg was standing with his eyes closed and smiling into the microphone.

"*. . . play a song for the lovers . . .*"

I looked up at him from below. He opened his eyes and looked down. He smiled and watched me as he sang. Then he climbed down off the stage and came up to me.

"How's things?" he asked.

I shrugged.

"Okay . . ."

"So what do you think of us?"

Us? The drummer and the bass player were crashed out in the bathroom. I liked Oleg okay. But not them.

"Fantastic," I answered.

"I get it." Oleg nodded and wrinkled up his nose.

"No, really, I did like it."

Oleg smiled and lit a cigarette. We sat on the stage without speaking. Masha Nikonova watched us from across the club, smiling to herself about Steklov.

*   *   *

I got covered in ketchup. Because the sausage kept falling out of the bread. They were running "Big in Japan" on the TV. *"Things will happen while they can, I will wait here for my man tonight . . ."* and all that stuff. I put the kettle on. Then I started drinking coffee. With honey cakes.

If anyone had told me a year ago that I'd be drinking coffee, I wouldn't have believed it. Coffee was my number one enemy ever since I was a kid. It used to make me feel sick, just like semolina did.

After the club, we all went to Sashka Berdyshev's place to sleep. We left the drummer behind in the club's restroom.

Everyone slept where they could. Masha somehow managed to squeeze herself onto two stools standing between the wardrobe and the sofa. Nastya and Galya slept on the table. And Kostya slept in the bathroom.

Four of us clambered onto the sofa. Oleg was breathing in my ear. Then he whispered:

"Are you asleep?"

"Nah," I whispered back.

"Want some candy?"

"Yeah!"

We sucked sticky fruit drops and felt happy, like partners in crime. Oleg smelled of apples and cigarette smoke.

"So where did you go?" I asked.

"Er . . ." Oleg waved his hand vaguely in the air. "This girl said, 'Let's go to my place,' so I went. I was drunk . . ."

"You're a funny guy."

"Not funny, strange."

"Why strange?"

"Because."

Oleg rummaged in his pocket and pulled out a guitar pick.

"Look, it's from New York."

"Really?" I didn't believe him.

"My friend brought it back for me. Fantastic, eh?"

"Yeah. And what did your friend bring for himself?"

"A guitar . . . the kind of guitar you could die for. I just fell in love with it!"

"With a guitar?"

Oleg nodded and sighed.

"Sing me something of your own," I said to him.

"How can I? Everybody's asleep. And the guitar . . ."

"Just sing it. In my ear."

"In your ear?"

He whispered the songs in my ear like poems. And it felt good, safe, like being in a bomb shelter.

Then I fell asleep. And Oleg fell asleep. And probably carried on singing in his sleep too.

I washed the dishes. On the radio Zemfira was searching for someone. And then Britney Spears was going insane. The phone rang insistently.

"Are you coming?" Oleg asked.

"I've got things to do."

Why the hell should I go anywhere?

"What's up, can't be bothered? Do I have to get down on my knees and crawl, or what?"

"People don't owe anybody anything anyway," I said.

"They don't," he agreed. "And you still haven't understood a single thing."

And he hung up.

2

The sky instantly turned dark and the leaves on the birch tree that had been fluttering loudly in the breeze froze, as if they were drawn in India ink on dark-blue Whatman paper. There was a sudden, sharp smell of damp bird-cherry blossom and sheet-iron windowsill. Another gust of wind, even stronger, was on its way, but it was forestalled by a rhythmic tapping on metal, followed by a rustling sound.

The heavy drops plunked onto the glazed surface of the page and soaked into it. Masha looked up. Outside the window the rain was pouring down gaily and the trees were swaying their branches in confusion under the bombardment. Masha wiped her nose with the edge of the bedspread, climbed off the bed and opened the window. The wind and rain burst into the room, the curtain bellied out like a sail and a few more drops of water fell onto the glazed pages. Masha stood there for a moment, shivering. She sniffed hard to stop her nose running and wiped her eyes. The rain drummed on the windowsill. Masha went into the bathroom and took the scissors out of the cabinet. She looked at her left wrist. At the plump blue-gray vein under the bluish skin. At her curving nails gleaming crimson like fruit drops, with shimmering hieroglyphs. Masha began cutting them with the big scissors, leaving stubby square ends. She cleaned off the varnish. Then she took a strand of hair, painstakingly waved and dyed with blue ink. Cut it off and tossed it into the sink. Then she looked at herself in the mirror and started crying. Her nose was running and the tears fell across the flush on her cheeks. The hair kept falling to the floor. Eventually Masha put the scissors back in the cabinet and turned on the tap. She threw the colored strands in the trash and stood there for a long time, massaging her face with cold water. Then she pulled a T-shirt with frills over her head. Put on a skirt that hugged her angular hips. She took a look at herself in the mirror then—skinny, pale, flat-chested. Different. Someone Else. She bit her lips and sat down in the corner of the bathroom, pressing herself against the cold tiles.

Steklov had told her: "Stop chasing after me, OK? Even if you bought up every shop Sisley and Benetton have, it wouldn't change a thing. Understand?"

But she didn't understand. It was impossible to imagine that everything could collapse so easily and the ground could twist out from under her feet like that. Laughing, mocking her.

The phone rang and Masha got up, but instead of answering it, she went to the wardrobe where all the things she didn't need anymore were gathering dust. She pulled out the old jeans, worn colorless, that she used to wear two years ago, and her younger sister Katka's dark green T-shirt. The socks were there too, in the corner. Then Masha fished her keys and two ten-ruble notes out of her handbag. She slipped her feet into the sneakers her father used for gardening, gray with ingrained dirt. She slammed the door behind her.

The rain greeted her with bubbles floating on the puddles. The thick summer air was intoxicating, heavy with the scent of plants and flowers. Mauve-gray bunches of lilac hung in profusion, giving off a piercing perfume. Masha stood on the porch for a moment, then set off down the street. It was already dark and the reflections of the street-lights were yellow blots in the shiny black of the asphalt. Masha walked through the puddles and her sneakers turned instantly black. The raindrops mingled with her tears and ran down the back of her neck. Steklov's words ran through her head like a tape on a loop: " . . . it wouldn't change a thing . . . it wouldn't change a thing . . ."

Masha reached the bus stop and sat on the bench under the shelter. She shivered. Her hair had clumped into icicles and her sneakers were so wet they weighed her feet down, pressing them onto the asphalt. A woman came up to her and asked what time it was.

"Eleven o'clock," Masha answered.

The woman pointed toward a nearby phone booth.

"They're taking the money . . . They've got it in that bag of theirs . . ."

Masha craned her neck and saw the bag. She nodded to be polite.

"They collect the money and take it away," the woman went on. "All this time I've been living here—thirty years—and still they keep taking it."

Masha doubted that the phone booth attendants had been carrying money around here for thirty years. But she decided not to say anything.

"Forty years I've been living here," said the woman, pointing at the phone booth. "And they've got all that money, what do they need it all for . . ."

She's an alcoholic, thought Masha.

"They slit open my handbag," the women suddenly confided in her. "Took out my passport and pension book . . ." Her voice began to tremble. "Two years ago it was . . ."

"You can get a new passport," said Masha.

"And a pension book . . . Five thousand for a passport . . . Six thousand for a pension book . . . I haven't got any money." The woman fluttered her hands and muttered. "My son threw me out of the house, the rat. Says, did you get your pension, you old bitch? Takes the money and drinks it all . . . The bastard . . . He's got a big ugly red face, and great big black circles like that under his eyes, you can't even see his eyes . . . I'll have him thrown out of the apartment. Send him to hell. I'll go to Weiner Street and have him evicted . . . And then I'll go to the police . . . Some time behind bars will teach him a thing or two . . ."

"How old is your son?" Masha asked.

"Eighteen."

Steklov's twenty, thought Masha. And I'm seventeen . . .

The number fifty bus drew up. Masha got to her feet.

"Goodbye."

The woman gave her a toothless smile. Masha pulled money out of her pocket and thrust it into the woman's hand. The woman looked at her, baffled.

"What?" she mumbled in confusion, but when she saw the two ten-ruble notes in the light of the street lamps, she smiled again.

Masha hopped onto the bus. She looked around. It was bright and warm inside, and there weren't too many people.

Sitting not far away was a fat granny with a red face in a cotton print dress. Her plump hands, stained dark with earth, grasped two bags containing seedlings in old milk and kefir cartons. Sitting in front of her was a young father with glasses and a pale, exhausted face. A plump four-year-old girl was sleeping on his knees in a white summer hat and tights. Her polka-dot dress was tucked straight into the top of the tights. The girl was clutching a withered branch of white lilac in one hand. Sitting beside them was a boy with earphones on his shaved head. Raindrops glistened on the fuzzy surface. The conductor approached Masha.

"What are you paying with?" the conductor asked.

Masha started in embarrassment and said nothing.

The conductor waited.

"Nothing," Masha mumbled.

The conductor peered at her.

"Well, never mind then . . ."

Masha looked at the conductor and sighed. The conductor responded with a half smile of her painted pink lips. Masha leaned her hot forehead against the glass of the window. The shaven-headed boy glanced around at her with a glint of whitish eyelashes.

Masha got out in the center of town. There was still plenty of life here; couples strolled and car headlights flashed by. Masha set off along an avenue without bothering to think where she was going. The rain was still splashing and gurgling in the drains.

"Hello there, darling."

There were two guys standing in front of her—one thickset and fleshy-faced and the other slimmer, looking like Roman Jagupov from the band Zdob Si Zdub.

"Hello," said Masha uncertainly.

"What are you doing out all alone so late?" asked the fleshy-faced one.

Masha gave a noncommittal shrug. Zdob Si Zdub smoked, squinting his eyes.

"But where are you going?" the fleshy-faced one persisted.

Masha gave another shrug.

"Come back to our place," Zdob Si Zdub suggested and

laughed when he saw Masha twitch in alarm. "Don't be afraid. We're not maniacs."

The fleshy-faced one laughed too. Masha looked from one to the other, not knowing what to do.

"Let's go," Zdob Si Zdub said again.

"No thanks," Masha replied, getting a sudden vision of newspaper headlines—*She was only seventeen.*

"A pity. A great pity," said the fleshy-faced one, shaking his head. "Can we walk you somewhere?"

"No!" Masha cried out. Zdob Si Zdub smiled.

"Okay, have it your way . . ."

Masha walked away quickly, then started running. She almost knocked some woman off the pavement with her elbow.

"Young man!" the woman protested loudly.

"Not an ounce of respect," said an old man carrying a sack of bottles, with a shake of his head.

Masha stopped in front of the Lenin monument, breathing heavily. She glanced around. There was no one chasing her. Cursing herself for being so easily scared, Masha sat down on the stone steps. They were wet and she jumped back up. Then she heard someone say:

"Masha? Masha Nikonova?"

Standing there in front of her holding a bottle of beer was a student from her year, Sashka Berdyshev. Masha smiled happily.

"Hi!"

"Hi," said Sashka, looking her over uncertainly. She looked more like Taylor Hanson now than Masha Nikonova. "Is it really you?"

"Yep." She thought that was funny.

"We-ell." Sashka scratched the back of his head and said, "Why don't you come to our party?"

"Okay."

They walked for a long time through courtyards, along alleys. Sashka's pager beeped twice to tell him which way to go and both times it was wrong. Masha was tired and wet. Sashka held her hand and dragged her along after him like a child. When they finally reached the entrance to the house, the metal door was closed. Sashka whistled and shouted "Lyo-okha!" and Masha laughed loudly, giving Sashka a fright. But then they both laughed together and finished the bottle of beer as they sat on the wet railings. Half an hour later they were let in.

Everyone who knew Masha was amazed at her appearance, but most were strangers who took her for a boyish girl. Not the worst possible image to have.

Masha squeezed in between a punk girl and a boy who was naked to the waist and dead drunk. They were singing songs, drinking vodka, smoking and laughing. Masha laughed and smoked too, and the punk girl fell asleep on her shoulder. Sashka took Oleg's guitar and started singing: *I think I'll sing a song abou-out love* . . .

"Hello . . ."

Masha turned around and saw Steklov.

"Hi," she said in a husky voice. Her throat was suddenly so tight it hurt.

"That's crazy," said Steklov, looking at her hair in amazement.

Masha nodded, incapable of saying a single word.

"I didn't really expect to see you here," said Steklov.

"Me neither . . ." Masha forced the words out and bit her lip. She swallowed, forcing the tears back inside. She suddenly felt dizzy, wanted to scream.

Masha wriggled out from under the sleeping girl and

went to the kitchen. She pressed her head against the glass and began to cry. Bitterly, as if she were at a funeral.

"What's wrong?" she heard someone whisper.

Standing beside her was a young guy in a red shirt, holding out a glass of water in sympathy.

"Nothing," Masha wiped her face with the hem of her T-shirt and took the glass. "Thank you."

She started to drink. Her throat constricted.

The guy suddenly said: "I've seen you somewhere before." Masha looked at him.

"I've seen you too." Masha gave a deep sigh and it became easier to breathe. He held out his hand:

"Aren't you . . .? I'm Vova."

"Masha . . . You . . . you look like Roman Jagupov out of Zdob Si Zdub."

Vova wrinkled up his nose and smiled the way people do when they hear something that they've heard too many times, but don't say anything because they want the other person to like them.

3

Anton crawled out of the apartment in the early morning and went to the bread shop. The sun had risen before him and it shone savagely into his eyes. He squinted, rubbed his face and swore under his breath.

He bought a long loaf and four bottles of beer, then set off back to the apartment. He almost fell asleep in the elevator, but was roused by the stench of urine. Inside the apartment there were five or six people sleeping next to each other in a row. Anton prodded the nearest one with his foot.

A fair, curly-haired guy in a yellow shirt stirred in annoyance and mumbled something incomprehensible.

"Oleg," said Anton. "Let's have a drink. I've bought some bread too."

Oleg gave a wide yawn and sat up on the floor. He forced his eyes open and looked at Anton in astonishment.

"What's up with your ear?"

Anton touched the dark brown lump of congealed blood on his left earlobe and said in a mystified voice:

"Someone's torn my earring off . . ."

They went into the kitchen. Oleg put the kettle on and looked in the cupboard for coffee. Anton sat on the windowsill and lit up. Oleg sniffed the air and glanced back over his shoulder.

"This early in the morning?"

"So what?" Anton snarled back, trying to hide the joint. His fingers were shaking and he dropped it. He bent down and picked it up quickly.

Oleg said nothing and sat down to wait for the water to boil. He took his guitar and began strumming something. Anton brightened up and began clumsily singing along. He didn't know the words, so he fidgeted on the windowsill and howled:

"*La-la-la . . . na-na . . . hey-hey . . .*" Then he scratched his nose and asked: "That's The Verve, isn't it?"

"Richard Ashcroft, on his own . . ."

"Aha, sure, I know it . . . Er, er . . . 'A Song for Lovers' . . . I've seen it . . ."

The kettle began whistling. Oleg put down the guitar and poured boiling water into two mugs, stirring in the coffee.

"I won't have any," Anton said hastily. "I'll have a beer . . ."

"Drink it."

"Ah, okay . . . Yeah . . . No problem . . ."

They sat at the table and drank coffee.

"We're playing at the Swineherd today," said Oleg.

"Your brains fucked or something? We're playing there on Friday."

"You're the one whose brains are fucked. Today's Friday."

Anton looked at the tear-off calendar hanging by the sink. He read "Tuesday."

"Today's Tuesday," he said, poking the calendar with his finger.

Oleg looked at the top sheet.

"Read the date, dickhead."

"Eighteenth of January," Anton read out. He looked through the window—out there the branches of the maple were swaying, rustling their leaves. He looked at the calendar again. Written in pencil above the date it said: "Dima, I want you." Who's Dima? thought Anton.

Oleg suddenly froze, with the mug held to his mouth; then his eyes swivelled rapidly upward and bored into Anton's.

"What?" Anton asked in fright.

"We've got Russian today. Fuck."

"Fuck it," Anton agreed. "And I don't know shit. But when is it? Nine, eh?"

Oleg nodded.

"No need to freak out just yet, then," Anton reassured him. "It's only half past seven."

A disheveled-looking girl with a puffy face and swollen lips came into the kitchen. Her eyes looked dull and bleary—she obviously hadn't taken her mascara off the night before. The girl opened a bottle of beer and sat on Oleg's knees.

"Ryabova," said Oleg, pushing her off unceremoniously, "sit over there on the chair, will you?"

Svetka Ryabova got up, looked around in surprise, then looked at herself and began scraping the white stains off her T-shirt. Anton chortled.

"Who were you with last night?" asked Oleg, lighting a cigarette. He closed his eyes and blew out smoke to one side.

"Anton."

"I don't remember," Anton confessed.

"Well you can fuck off then."

Anton ignored that, reached for a cigarette and stuck it in Svetka's mouth. She nodded.

The three of them sat there smoking in silence and Anton tried to remember what he'd been up to the night before. Especially what had happened with Svetka. Then he remembered that the band had a gig today and he started thinking about that instead. He thought he ought to get washed up and headed to the bathroom, locking the door behind him.

Oleg and Svetka sat in the kitchen without speaking. Svetka looked at Oleg and he looked out through the window at the maple. Svetka was thinking it would have been better to let Oleg have her. But Oleg didn't want her. Even if he got totally smashed, he still wouldn't take her. Svetka remembered how at one party she'd said to Oleg: "I love you," and he'd looked at her like she was an idiot. He'd gone into the kitchen. Sat in the same place he was sitting now and smoked. Then they'd sat there with Yulka Mukhina, Svetka's friend, and Svetka had gotten drunk and all the guys had taken turns with her. It was what she'd wanted herself. Ah, fuck it . . .

Anton came out of the bathroom, naked and wet. He walked into the kitchen, rummaged in the cupboards and looked under the table. Svetka looked at the knobbly vertebrae on his thin back and over it the huge writhing dragon, its scaly tail lying in rings. Anton straightened up and Svetka could see that both of his nipples and his navel were pierced. Beautiful, thought Svetka, nodding her head.

"Oleg, have you seen the towel anywhere?" Anton asked.

"Sanya's sleeping on it."

Anton nodded and went into the room. A moment later they heard Sashka Berdyshev yelling:

"And I'm the coolest. And clearly the best looking!"

Anton didn't understand anything on the Russian test. He sat at his desk, trying to figure out which part of a sentence was the subject and which was the predicate. Then he fell asleep. Oleg nudged him awake when the teacher called him up to the front of the class. He took a sheet of paper with him and read out all the notes Oleg had scribbled rapidly on the paper ten minutes earlier. He was awarded a "satisfactory." He took his student record book and went out into the corridor for a smoke. Nastya Kulakova walked by.

"Nast!" Anton called out to her.

"What?"

She came over, knitting her brows, tossing her dark brown hair. Anton pulled her close to him and kissed her on the lips, desperately, as if he was about to burst into tears. Nastya grabbed him around the neck with both hands and said:

"You're a fool, Anton, what a stupid fool you are . . ."

Anton nodded, choking in the thick pink haze that was enveloping him, drawing him down into some sweet abyss, setting his head spinning.

"Why didn't you come yesterday?" he asked hoarsely, stubbing his cigarette out on the wall.

"For what?" said Nastya, emphasizing the second word. Anton said nothing. He didn't understand.

"You know what, Anton," she said suddenly. "Let's just be friends, okay?"

"What d'you mean?" He was confused. "You're dumping me, is that it?"

"No, well I suppose yes . . . I'm not dumping you . . . Just let's be friends, that's all . . ."

Slowly, Anton pulled a cigarette out of his pocket, lit it, took a drag and only then said:

"If that's what you want."

"Right, that's great!"

Nastya kissed him noisily on the lips, then turned and walked away.

"Nast!" Anton called, as if he'd just woken up.

She looked round, annoyed.

"We're playing the Swineherd today. Are you going to come?"

She turned back and walked on without answering. Anton sat down against the wall and burst into tears.

At the Swineherd the air was thick with smoke and it smelled of alcohol with a strange hint of lilac. Oleg stood onstage with his guitar and sang, almost shouting. Seryoga sat on a speaker, his bass in his arms and his legs dangling. Anton hammered away violently on the drums, yelling out occasional words. His stomach was rumbling and his head was buzzing. He shook his head about, trying to thrash the noise out of it, but he couldn't, and he squeezed the drumsticks so tight his hands hurt.

You waited for me, but you got too tired,
I tried to catch the moments, hold them in my hand,
You gave up and you left just for a while
But now you don't want to come back again . . .

sang Oleg, pressing his lips against the microphone.

You screwed someone, I'm ready to forgive,
You kissed someone not me, but what,
As you lay on his chest, what did you think?
You told me that I spoil your life, spoil everything,

sang Anton, joining in.

But without you, I'll die,
Do you know that?
I don't know how to hold you back . . .
I'll simply die,
Don't fly away, don't fly . . .
I don't know how to hold you back, when I spoil everything.

Seryoga sang in almost childish amazement, as though the lines were something he'd only just discovered that very moment and he still hadn't figured out how he was supposed to feel about them.

Anton suddenly felt a pain in his elbows, as though someone had twisted and broken them like a roasted chicken leg. He bit his lip and carried on playing, but he stopped singing. He felt a salty taste in his mouth. He wiped his lips on his sleeve and looked in surprise at the dark streak they left there. Oleg turned to look at him and pulled a terrible face. Anton hastily counted out "one, two, three," with his drumsticks and started hammering away:

> *You didn't want to hurt me, you just left,*
> *You said that I never loved you at all,*
> *Tell me, who were you lying to that time,*
> *When you didn't believe a word yourself . . .*

he sang in a quavering voice.

> *And I didn't believe it either,*

said Seryoga with conviction.

> *You walked the dark alleys on your own,*
> *I wasn't there, I thought it was right,*
> *I made the rules and then pretended there were none*
> *But I believed, I knew that you were there . . .*

whispered Oleg, pressing his lips against the microphone.

After their set the next band came out onstage. Seryoga switched off right away and Oleg stared glassy-eyed at the stage, tapping out the rhythm on the wall with his finger. Anton was sober, thinking about Nastya. He spent a lot of time just getting high, but he still managed to write a few songs, and they were all about Nastya. Only now he couldn't sing them. He just couldn't, physically. He remembered how they'd made love beside Oleg when he was asleep, and then laughed all day because he hadn't noticed or heard anything. And how he'd once spent the night at Nastya's place and her vigilant mother had come into the room every hour. But they'd just been talking, Nastya snuggled under the blanket on the bed and Anton sitting on the sofa. They'd talked about the Beatles and Hands Up!, about Pelevin and Tokareva, about the Internet, about dogs, sex, space, about when they and their friends were children, about their relatives and vodka and the band that Anton had only just begun to play in. It was the most incredible night in his whole life.

Two girls came up and sat beside him, looking about fifteen or sixteen. One of them was wearing bright lipstick, but it was still obvious she was underage. The other was pale and small with slim fingers and transparent ears. Fans, thought Anton. Oleg started talking crap, making himself out to be a big shot, and the girls gaped at him in admiration. It made Anton laugh. The skinny girl looked at him, at first in surprise, but then her face took on a kind of adoring, available look, and she grabbed hold of Anton's hand. He pulled it away as if he'd been scalded and jumped to his feet. Oleg watched him go with a sad expression and then turned back to the girls.

Anton came out of the club and set off down the street with his hands stuck in his pockets. He walked along the middle of the road, past the cars that rushed by furiously sounding their horns. But he couldn't care less. He was better off dead anyway. He already was dead. And now he was flying up into the air with his tattooed arms flung wide and his head thrown back and his tears falling down, glittering like the morning dew in the light of the street lamps. He sang: "La-la-la-la . . . na-na . . . hey-hey!" and laughed so he wouldn't start crying and fall. He grabbed hold of a windowsill and felt a powerful blow that smacked him against the brick wall. His nipples and navel started hurting where the rings had been pressed into the skin. There was a smell of wet metal windowsills and bird-cherry blossom. He felt thirsty. He wanted to hear Nastya's voice. He turned off into the next side street, and went into a battered telephone booth with broken panes of glass and a dim little lightbulb. He rummaged through his pockets, but all he found was some grass wrapped in a piece of paper, so he began punching in numbers on the off chance it would work. First one ring then another drifted away into infinity; then there was a click and Anton heard her voice, tight with irritation:

"Are you coming?"

"I've got things to do!" was the sharp reply.

"What's up, can't you be bothered? Do I have to get down on my knees and crawl?"

"Okay, okay, I'm coming now, calm down . . ."

The line started beeping. Anton stood there for a moment with the phone pressed to his ear, then carefully put it back on the hook. He walked out of the booth, looking around, and set off quickly toward the bus stop. It was cold. A sudden gust of wind made him shiver. A few drops of rain fell on his nose, burning like ice. There was a crash of thunder and then the rain came down in a solid wall. Anton swore abruptly, raised his collar and ran for the stop. The bus slammed its doors shut in his face, hissed and moved off. Anton spat in annoyance and went under the shelter. There was a woman in a green raincoat sitting there, staring straight ahead of her. Anton sat a little distance away from her and starting thinking about Nastya. He couldn't get his head straight. It was as if some door in his brain were locked. Anton shook his head and the woman began muttering as if she'd just woken up:

"I should be going . . . but what for? . . . I'll have the pig arrested . . . let the bastard do some time, that'll teach him."

Anton got up and started walking. His elbows hurt. His back was cold, as though someone had fixed their eyes on him from behind and was staring, staring, staring . . . Anton came to a building, hesitated for a moment and went into the entranceway. He sat on the cold steps and rolled a joint. Then he closed his eyes blissfully and saw a sticky pink cloud. His throat contracted as if he was choking. Someone had grabbed him by the back of the neck and smashed him over the head with something heavy. Anton opened his eyes for a moment and caught a glimpse of a greasy red face, a mustache and bald patch.

"Fucking junkie," the red face whispered in a deep bass.

Anton felt frightened and at the same moment he felt someone tearing his ears off. He yelled, feeling his throat rip open and blood flood into his mouth. He choked and fell, sinking into a pink haze . . .

He woke up in a puddle, lying on broken bricks. He lay there for a minute, trying to figure out what had happened, then felt his head. It was sticky at the back, and his left ear was stinging and dangling like jelly, with blood dripping from the tatters. Anton got up and started walking. He ran into a rough wall, turned around and went back. Rain gurgled in a drainpipe.

4

Heat pushed through the window, and succulent greenery swarmed over the yards and threatened to creep through the open gap. The cat had been lying peacefully on the bed. It stretched, pushing out its fluffy belly, and gave Galya a foul look. Galya returned the stare and the cat turned away pensively. The speakers standing on the table were pounding and the room was filled with song: *"So give me coffee and TV . . ."* Galya kept blinking, but her eyes stung anyway. The sun was fresh, only just up and unbearably bright. Galya swore as she squinted her eyes. *"I'm going blind and I'm brain dead virtually . . ."* She'd been in a chat room all night, so her head was throbbing and fit to burst. She met three guys on-line, although right now she didn't feel like seeing anyone. She didn't want to go anywhere; she didn't want the hassle of waiting around, swapping life stories. She chased the cat-creature off the bed where it had fallen asleep and instantly fell into a deep sleep herself. The cat took its chance to gnaw on Galya's feet and sit on her head for a while before finally stretching out beside her and falling asleep again.

Galya dreamed she was jumping from house to house like a character in *The Matrix*. It took her breath away and her heart skipped a beat when she flew up into the air. She woke up at four o'clock, when the sun had already turned the air incandescent and scorched the leaves, making them give off a sickly-sweet aroma. She remembered her dream and thought: It means I'm growing.

There was nowhere left for Galya Romanova to grow. At 5'9" she towered over the girls in her year and even over some of the boys. She didn't want to be a model; she could never cope with the restricted diet and other hassles of a model's life. She didn't want to be a basketball player either—she didn't like basketball.

So Galya's height was never put to good use. And men didn't exactly fall at her feet in droves, either, preferring girls a little shorter. But Galya didn't get too worked up about it; she'd gotten used to making do with two or three childhood friends. The others were "just acquaintances."

The phone rang, disturbing the cat, who growled in annoyance and got up to pee. Galya picked up the receiver.

It was Steklov. She loved Steklov the way she loved her cat. He was cheerful and pleasant. (The cat wasn't cheerful and pleasant, but they shared the same status as objects of affection—Galya didn't love the cat and Steklov "liked guys.") They called each other and sometimes met up at the Dam to eat ice cream. Steklov told her about his life. Galya told him about hers. They went to each other's birthday parties, skipped classes together and sent e-mails. Galya could see that some of the girls in her year were in love with Steklov and that made her laugh. Lots of things made her laugh.

"Have you written the essay?" Steklov asked.

"Nah . . . I was on the Net. I'll never get the damn thing written."

"Why don't I send you mine?"

"Who'd you write it for?"

"Lopukhov."

"I'm doing it for Lopukhov too. Do you think he's got Alzheimer's? If he finds out . . ."

"Rework it a bit then."

"Nah," Galya whined. "Steklov, I can't be bothered! You can't imagine what a drag it is!"

"I can imagine," Steklov said. "And I suppose you've still got the English exam to come . . ."

"I'll pass it . . . There's three whole days left till English! Hey, Steklov, let's go out somewhere, eh? I'm bored."

Steklov thought for a while, then he said:

"Well . . . the thing is . . . I met this girl today and we're going . . . I'm sorry, Galya . . . Some other time, okay?"

"Oh yeah? What kind of girl?"

"A nice one. Clever and beautiful. Her name's Dasha."

"I'm insanely happy for you," Galya said in a voice from beyond the grave.

"Galya, don't take offense!"

"I won't," Galya promised. "Goodbye, my darling."

"Bye!"

The cat came back from the bathroom, sat on a chair and stared at the wall.

"Puss, puss . . ." Galya called.

The cat slowly turned its head, nodded as if to say, I appreciate the gesture, and turned back to the wall again. Then it made a sudden dash forward, grabbed a cockroach and ate it, grimacing in disgust.

"Are you short on vitamins or something?" Galya yelled.

The cat got angry and bit Galya's foot, then went out onto the balcony and sat there on the rail, waiting for the next-door neighbors' six-year-old Vanechka to poke his hand through to stroke it, so that it could stick its claws into the hand and bite it. The cat obviously had the soul of a dog. Or a horse.

Galya sat down at her computer, but she didn't feel like going into the chat room, so she checked her e-mails. There were three messages from the Foo Fighters fan club, one from a girlfriend in Israel and one from Steklov. He wrote: "Sunshine ☺ I got a three for literature . . . are you going to console me? Ha-ha! ☺ On Saturday there's a gig on at the Dam, we can go if you like. Otherwise everything's fine, drop the ram into the dean's office tomorrow, I need to unzip a clip . . . OK? that's it, cheers, Pasha. ☺ "

Galya smiled and thought that perhaps she should meet those three guys after all. They called themselves Neo, Wild-WildDen and Busta. Galya was Cleo. Steklov sometimes even called her that in school. No one else there could understand why he said: "Hi, Cleo!" And why Galya answered: "Hey, Pepper!" The girls who were in love with Steklov squinted at her in annoyance. They called Steklov Pasha or Pavlik and they didn't like Galya.

The cat came in from the balcony, cozied up to Galya and fell asleep on her knees.

5

Masha Nikonova came out of the bathroom and set off toward the dacha, adjusting her shorts. There the smell of smoke and kebabs hung in the air, which was light and fresh, free of buzzing mosquitoes and popular fluff. It was sheer heaven. Masha turned toward the barbecue and started in surprise. Steklov was standing by the fire with his back toward her, dousing the kebabs with a mixture of water and wine from a battered plastic bottle. His naked back rippled with almost childlike muscles; he'd turned up the bottoms of his black jeans and looked rather comical, as if he were someone else, not Steklov at all. But it was Steklov, as natural as always. Shifting his bare feet in those sandals as he turned the spits.

Masha stood motionless for a while, then walked a little distance away and sat on a folding chair. She was just sitting there. That was allowed, wasn't it? She had a deep sinking feeling in her stomach, like everything was falling into a cold abyss.

Steklov was singing something to himself and swaying his hips. Like a gay man, thought Masha. She sat there and watched Steklov's back, his curly hair and his backside. Beautiful. Steklov glimpsed her out of the corner of his eye and turned around. Masha stared intently at a currant bush off to one side.

Steklov turned away again, but his movements were less free now. In order not to feel awkward, caught in the sights of Masha's gaze, he started singing his little song again. Masha could just catch the words: *"Sweat baby sweat baby sex is a Texas drought . . ."* After a while, as if he were addressing the empty air, Steklov said:

"The kebabs are almost ready . . ." as if he wasn't talking to Masha, but himself. "We'll just turn them over one last time . . ."

It took Masha's breath away that the man she loved and hated so violently was talking to her so gently, almost affectionately. The smell of roasting meat tickled her nostrils.

Steklov picked up a spit, turned toward Masha and spoke into the empty air again:

"It should be ready now . . ."

Masha stayed where she was, with her eyes glued to the currant bush. She suddenly felt herself slip back to her old self, her old life, where everything was hopeless, dark and empty, when she kept bumping into damp gray walls all the time and screaming, but her voice faded away to nothing under the vaults of the stone box. She tossed the hair back off her forehead—it had fallen forward again and was dangling in front of her eyes. Masha looked like a handsome boy. Steklov watched her, holding the spit in his hand. Then he put it back down and stood indecisively beside the barbecue for a while, assessing Masha with his black eyes. She stared hard at the ground. Steklov suddenly came over and squatted down in front of her. Masha gasped for air when she caught his smell and felt his warmth and his glance so close. Steklov said nothing; he didn't know what to say. Finally he blurted out:

"What's wrong?"

"Nothing," Masha answered sharply, barely able to hold back the tears. Then suddenly she sobbed and said:

"Go away."

Steklov didn't move.

Sashka and Galya came out of the house with plates of tomatoes and cucumbers. Masha jumped to her feet, throwing Steklov a frightened look. He recoiled too, and apart from the fright Masha could read incomprehension in his eyes: What the fuck? Sashka set down the tomatoes on the table and inquired cheerfully:

"Well, how are the kebabs?"

"Ready," Steklov replied in the same cheerful tone and smiled at Galya, who blushed, but still gave him a look of affected indignation. Now it was Masha's turn to think: What the fuck?

Sashka, Steklov, Galya, Masha and seven other people sat around the fire, eating kebabs with beer and vodka. The logs on the fire crackled, the cucumbers crunched and Lyokha Petrov got tomato juice and seeds on his T-shirt. Masha sat so she couldn't see Steklov, and he played the comic and cracked jokes, sending Galya and Yulka into gales of choking laughter. Nastya wasn't laughing; she was watching Steklov with a kind of intent indifference, and he kept stumbling over her glance. Oleg and Sashka were singing quietly: *"But if you've got some cigarettes in your pocket, it means things aren't so bad, at least today . . ."*

Svetka Ryabova was singing along and making Marinka Travkina frown. Then Steklov stopped talking and they all sang: *"Why don't I sing a song abou-out love . . ."* and *"You only forgot me for a couple of hours, and you don't even remember what happened yesterday . . ."* Galya's cat came over to the fire and tried to bite Kostya Patrushev to death, but he deftly caught it and threw it onto Lyokha Petrov. The cat dug its claws into Lyokha and it took them a long time to pull it off. When they did, it crawled across slyly to Svetka and gave her an aggressive bite on the finger, then fled the scene.

Masha quietly got up and went first to the bathroom and then out through the gate, to the river. It was already quite cold and she could feel the freshness from the water . . . The air was cooling in layers: higher up it was still dense and warm, but on the ground it was already cool, and Masha's feet felt the chill. The pure twilight, contrasting with the golden stripe on the horizon, embraced her and lulled her. She could smell the smoke of stoves burning on the opposite bank and hear boys talking, fish splashing, dogs barking. After a while she heard cautious footsteps behind her and a moment later someone sat down beside her. Masha turned her head and saw Oleg's curls glowing gold in the final pale pink rays of the sunset. He took a cigarette from behind his ear and lit it, looking at the river. On the opposite bank a voice called out clearly:

"Kolya, home!"

"Coming . . ."

Oleg smiled and looked at Masha. She smiled too. Then they sat there in silence, looking at the wispy clouds and listening to the sounds coming from the opposite bank. A car sounded its horn, dogs immediately started barking in cheerful fury, someone shouted and then there was laughter and a child's voice declared loudly: "That's not how I do it!" The car engine rattled into motion; the dogs that had just calmed down all started barking again, but then immediately fell silent. There was a long, drawn-out "Moo-oo-oo," then a splash and a woman shouted:

"Kolya, come out of the water this instant!"

Oleg flicked his cigarette butt away, took off his shirt and threw it across Masha's shoulders. Two dogs approached them: one big and shaggy with a broad, friendly face and soft eyes, the other skinny and fidgety, half the size of his companion, with ears that stuck out and a mean expression on its smooth, narrow face. The friendly-looking dog sat down not far away and the fidgety one came up to Oleg and Masha, fussing about and poking his nose against their hands and sniffing their pockets. Oleg took two biscuits out of his pocket and held one out to the fussy creature. It took it, squeamishly at first, and then ate it. Oleg threw the other to the friendly-looking dog, which wagged its tangled tail in gratitude. The skinny dog left immediately, followed by the friendly-looking one.

Masha laughed. Oleg chuckled too and stroked his hair.

"You've got burs," Masha remarked. He rolled his eyes.

Masha pulled his head down by the hair and started picking the prickly burs out of his curls. Oleg grimaced and gasped theatrically, and sometimes not so theatrically. Masha untangled the final bur, Oleg raised his head and they looked at each other. Masha felt a sweet trembling sensation as she looked at Oleg's lips and catlike eyes. He gave her a friendly smile and sat up the way he was sitting before. Masha stared at the water too, but now her head was swimming and her ears were burning. What's wrong with me, dammit? she thought in fright, pressing her legs up against her breasts and hugging them tight, as if she were trying to make herself smaller.

They heard talking and laughter on the path and Kostya and Yulka came out onto the riverbank.

Yulka exclaimed in delight.

"Oleg!" And then in the same voice: "Masha!"

"Hi!" Kostya sat down beside Oleg and Yulka sat beside Masha.

"Check it out: Sery got drunk again and locked himself in the bathroom!" Yulka announced cheerfully. "It's so funny! It's awful! And you missed it all!"

"Missed it?" laughed Oleg. "Sery does that every day, so you could say we've had a break from the daily routine."

Masha smiled and Yulka began to speak.

"But where's Anton?"

"I don't know," said Oleg with a shrug. "He said he'd come if he could."

"If he passed that damned military theory class?" chuckled Kostya.

"Yeah."

"Poor Anton! The moment Baranov sees his rings and tattoos, he'll throw him out."

"Let's hope not," said Oleg, with a sideways glance at Kostya, thinking he was hilarious. "They didn't throw you out, and I know you've got a tattoo on your chest. And one on your temple."

"Well, so what? So what? You can't see the one on my temple!" said Kostya, jumping to his feet, and they all laughed at his overreaction.

"Show us the one on your chest!" Yulka demanded.

Kostya happily pulled his T-shirt up over his head and Masha saw a tattoo of a tiger's head, and under it the words

"It's not my *problem."* The tiger had obviously been intended to look vicious, but Masha thought the expression on its face was a bit stupid. Kostya got dressed again, pleased with himself.

"Fantastic, fantastic," Yulka said approvingly, "but Anton's is classier."

They sat for a while without speaking. Then without saying a word, they got up and headed back to Galya's dacha. Fussy and Friendly suddenly appeared out of nowhere and started running along beside them, wagging their tails.

A fire was burning out in the yard of the dacha and everyone was sitting inside, playing cards. Just as Masha, Oleg, Yulka and Kostya arrived, Lyokha came running around the corner of the house, barking. Fussy and Friendly barked back at him and went away.

"Let's play for forfeits!" Lyokha blurted between his "woof-woofs" as he ran by.

"I want to play strip poker!" Kostya declared.

"Strip then!" someone advised him good-naturedly from the house.

Inside the house a cozy yellow light flooded the walls.

"Let's play spin the bottle!" suggested Svetka Ryabova.

"Yes, let's," said Yulka, offering unexpected support as she sat down beside Steklov.

"But let's not play for a kiss," said Lyokha, panting. "But for . . . you know . . . having sex."

"Fantastic!" said Marinka Travkina, with a look at Steklov, who shook his head in pretend disapproval.

"Yes, let's!" said Oleg, getting enthusiastic.

Everyone immediately voted for it, warming to the mixture of apprehension and risk.

They got an empty beer bottle and sat around the table in a circle.

"If it's a girl and a girl, do they . . . too?" asked Galya, glancing warily at the bottle.

"Nah, only if they want to . . ."

They switched on the radio—*"Crazy . . . I'm so into you!"* rumbled around the house. Kostya gave the bottle a spin. Masha felt everything in her belly tighten, leaving just her heart beating somewhere in her head.

"Svetka . . . and Marinka!" Kostya announced. "Well, are you up for it? Will you?"

"I don't think so," said Marinka, squinting at Svetka.

Kostya spun the bottle again. Oleg fidgeted on his chair and Lyokha suddenly sneezed and they all jumped because their nerves were already jangling, at full stretch.

"Steklov . . . and Oleg!"

"No, you're repulsive," said Steklov, dismissing Oleg. "Today's not your lucky day."

Everyone roared in relief. Kostya spun the bottle again and announced joyfully:

"Oleg and Masha!"

"Ho!" Steklov exclaimed.

Masha looked at Oleg with a bewildered smile.

"Go upstairs!" Nastya ordered them. She rummaged in the bag at her waist and pulled out a condom. "To make everything fair and square, come back with this . . ."

"Used," Lyokha prompted.

"Yeah!"

But isn't that rubber for Anton . . . thought Oleg. He stood up with Masha. They went upstairs and closed the door. It was dark and dusty in the room and somehow unnaturally quiet. They could hear the music from downstairs: *"You drive me crazy!"* Masha stood there looking dismayed in front of Oleg, and he sat down on the bed without saying anything. Then he asked:

"Well . . . what are we going to do?"

"I don't know," said Masha with a shrug.

"It feels stupid somehow . . ."

"Yeah . . ."

"Do you want to?"

Masha shrugged. Oleg sighed:

"Me too . . ."

Masha sat down beside him, terribly awkward. Oleg glanced sideways at her but didn't move. Then he suggested:

"Well . . . let's try a kiss, shall we . . ."

Masha shrugged again. She was suddenly overcome by the same trembling she'd felt not long ago on the bank of the river. They turned to face each other and kissed each other on the lips. Oleg focused intensely on his own sensations and sighed. They carried on sitting there in silence. Masha suddenly jumped up and ran out of the room, clattered down the stairs and slammed the door. Oleg got up, confused.

She ran along the path, choking on her tears, slipping on the grass and scratching her hands on the bushes. The path led her out to the riverbank. The blue-gray water was heaving majestically and it was quiet, with just an occasional splash or bark. Masha sat down on a log the fishermen used as a bench and lowered her head into her hands. She tried to figure out what had just happened. She knew that really nothing had happened, but her ears and cheeks were on fire and first Oleg, then Steklov kept flashing in front of her eyes.

"Damn the both of you!" Masha whispered in despair.

She heard noisy breathing and saw Fussy and Friendly

standing beside her, wagging their tails, smiling with their black jaws, their tongues lolling out.

Masha went back two hours later, with red, swollen eyes, her shorts covered in dog hair. Everyone in the dacha was asleep already. She walked quietly through to the room, saw a free place beside Yulka and lay down in it after she'd driven the cat away. It didn't resist, and didn't even try to give Masha a ferocious bite; in fact it starting purring and settled down at her feet.

"We didn't play anymore," Yulka suddenly whispered. "We started playing for kisses, but then we went back to playing cards for cash anyway . . ."

Masha nodded and Yulka smiled, turned to face the wall and fell asleep.

Masha looked around. Everybody was sleeping, breathing noisily. Galya Romanova had her arms round Kostya and Marinka had hers round Oleg. On the floor just in front of Masha, Steklov and Sashka Berdyshev were sleeping on sheepskin jackets. Steklov wrinkled up his nose in his sleep, breathing fitfully through lips that were half open like a child's. He'd put one hand under his cheek and he looked like a twelve-year-old. Stupid fool, thought Masha and closed her eyes.

She was on the point of falling asleep when she suddenly heard a cautious knock at the door. She listened. Everyone was asleep. There was another knock. *"Knock, knock Neo."*

Masha got up and walked over to the door. She went out into the hallway and pulled back the bolt.

Anton was standing on the doorstep, wrapped in a canvas jacket that was too big for him.

"Hello . . ." said Masha, bewildered.

"Hi," Anton replied quietly.

"Come in . . ."

Anton nodded seriously and came in, treading carefully. Masha closed the door and went into the room. She lay back down beside Yulka.

Anton looked around. Nastya was sleeping on an old sofa, huddled up in a rug. He sat beside her, then lay down and put his arm around her cautiously. As if he was afraid she'd wake up and send him away.

What's he doing? Masha thought in surprise.

Nastya started tossing about, then turned over and suddenly opened her eyes wide. She and Anton were lying so close their lips were touching. He went crazy; everything below his waist was tense and tight. Nastya stared at him in bewilderment for a while, but when Anton kissed her she came to her senses.

"Don't, Anton."

"Why not?" he whispered with plaintive passion.

"We're just friends now . . ."

"So what?"

"Friends don't do that."

Anton wanted to ask her what friends did do and if there were rules for friends written down somewhere—but instead he squeaked:

"I love you."

Nastya frowned and gingerly moved away.

"Anton, listen, there's someone else I like . . ."

Anton didn't understand at first, and then the meaning got through and he felt like he was falling down, down into the mud, scraping along the concrete walls of a well. Nastya saw him—"like a friend."

"What, for real?" Anton asked, choking.

"For real."

"Forever?"

Nastya nodded.

"What about me? What am I going to do?"

The despair was sucking Anton down. He tried to hang on to something, if only Nastya had at least said something . . . to give him hope, then he'd have something to cling to. But his hands were slipping, there was nothing to clutch at.

"I don't know what you're going to do."

Like an axe, smack across his hands! To finish the job.

"But you're . . ." Anton cried and stopped short. He wanted to say that Nastya meant more to him than anything else, that she was the only one who really understood him, that nobody could ever take her place, because . . . But the words got stuck somewhere in his chest. Nastya could only read them in his eyes. And she didn't want to.

Anton gave a shuddering sigh. Pressed his lips against Nastya's shoulder. Whispered:

"I'll die without you."

"I'm still with you. As a friend." Nastya stroked his hair. Cautiously, afraid of arousing his hopes.

"You promise?"

Nastya looked into his wide-open amber eyes with the wet lashes and said:

"I promise."

That was their most terrible oath. Anton felt better. Not much. But better. He slid off the sofa—friends don't sleep together—and sat on the floor. His shoulders smarted from being scraped along the concrete. His throat had gone dry. His stomach felt as if it had been crushed by rocks—but he could feel the pulse of "I'm still with you . . . I'm still with you . . ." I'm going to die, thought Anton. He was waiting for Nastya at least to stroke his hair, but she turned away and closed her eyes. Friends didn't stroke each other's hair. Nobody fucking knew what they were supposed to do.

6

Samson smelled of dog food. The smell made Svetka feel sick. Especially when he stuck his nose into her face in the morning and licked it with his long pink tongue as if he were wiping it with a rag. Samson's coat had a sour smell too, and in the morning it made Svetka gag.

The phone rang. Samson howled in delight and started barking loudly. Without opening her eyes, Svetka grabbed the receiver and put it to her ear.

"Hello . . ."

"It's me."

"Hi . . ."

"Hi. Have your folks gone to work yet?"

Svetka nodded into the pillow:

"Ughm . . ."

"I'll be right there."

"Mmnh . . ."

The phone started beeping rapidly. Svetka shoved it under the pillow.

She had to get out of bed, brush her teeth and wash. Seven o'clock . . . She had a foreign literature test at twelve. She could have slept until ten, but it was hard to make Seryoga understand that it was better to sleep than to screw.

Svetka crawled out of bed onto the floor. Samson wagged the stump of his tail happily. When he was a puppy they'd thought he was a black terrier and docked his tail. The passage of time had revealed that Samson was more like a German shepherd, but it was too late then to stitch his tail back on.

There was no hot water. The cold set her teeth on edge and the persistent taste of Signal toothpaste lingered in her mouth. Her hair was sticking out in all directions behind her ears and it was glued to the back of her head. Svetka smoothed the tufts down with water. Then she sprayed eau de toilette on her neck and applied anti-wrinkle cream to her cheeks and lips. There wasn't any other cream.

There wasn't any tea left either. And her mother had finished the remains of the coffee yesterday, when her dad left banging the door as if he wanted to smash it into pieces. Samson's aluminum bowl was standing beside the trash can with brown crumbs dried on around the edge. Mom had forgotten to put the sausage away in the fridge yesterday and now it had a greenish tinge. But Samson ate it happily.

Svetka took a long loaf of bread and went into the big room. She sat in front of the TV and switched it to channel five, MTV. "A party at D.T.'s place!" Svetka started picking pieces off the loaf and eating them.

She first met Seryoga at the entrance exams. They wrote an essay together. Then they stood in line for the history exam together. Seryoga was as pale as the white shirt he was wearing, and bald. His head was shaved, that is. It was immodestly naked and stubbly. He had forgotten his pen and Svetka gave him her spare. He never gave it back.

Svetka didn't do well enough to get in without fees and had to pay for tuition. Her mother had been livid.

Sery had gotten fifteen points and passed. He'd stood on the stairs smoking as if he wasn't even pleased. Svetka had stood beside him, feeling terribly embarrassed.

"What's your name?" Sery had asked.

"Svetka . . . Ryabova."

"I'm Sery."

It was right there on the same stairs that she'd met Oleg—he'd gotten fourteen points. So he'd passed too. Then it turned out Oleg was turned on by Oasis. And Sery was also turned on by Oasis. Svetka didn't know what it meant, but she said it turned her on as well. And Oleg had given her an interested look and Svetka had seen the color of his eyes—pure gold. And his golden curls. Damn . . .

Afterward Oleg and Sery had walked her to the bus stop. And they'd gone off together to drink beer. To celebrate the historic meeting, although then, of course, they hadn't known it was historic. It was just an excuse.

A month later they'd gotten their own band together and all of them started skipping classes to play in Sery's basement. Sery played bass and Oleg played lead guitar. Then they'd dreamed up this absolutely crazy song and everyone had gone around singing it. *The water leaks into the pink fluff, breathe in deep, fill your lungs—and then the veins burst . . . You'll never be mine and I'll never be yours!* That song made them stars at every party and Svetka had been proud that so far she was the only one who knew them "so well." And as quickly as that she fell in love with Oleg.

Eight o'clock . . . Svetka went into the bathroom and freshened up. Began outlining her eyes with the pencil. She had pale green eyes with whitish lashes. She felt sleepy. Sery still hadn't arrived. Svetka finished outlining her lips and started clearing the place up. She didn't want Sery to see the mess. She wanted him to think she was a good girl.

* * *

Oleg hadn't felt the same way about her, but Svetka hadn't done anything provocative anyway. Not for the time being at least. When she started seeing his curls on every street corner and she saw her status was gradually dropping from "a friend of the band" to "just another student," she decided to do something about it. She sat with Oleg in class and he saw her to the bus stop. But things never got beyond "Hi!—Hi!" Svetka consoled herself with the thought that Oleg was busy with the band and his studies. She was right about the band, but as for his studies—well, hardly.

He and Sery found themselves a drummer—always high on grass, a mass of holes and tattoos. They found him up at the back of the lecture hall. Anton. With Anton on board things started moving faster and soon they were getting invited to play gigs at clubs. They became real big shots. And they probably forgot about Svetka. Not that they'd ever thought about her much anyway.

Then one time the whole band had gone to a party at Anton's place. Svetka had gotten drunk and decided to risk it. She sat next to Oleg and said it, like she was diving into a whirlpool.

"Oleg . . . I . . . I love you."

Oleg had given her a puzzled look. She waited. He got up and went into the kitchen for a smoke.

It was the lowest moment of Svetka's seventeen years of life.

That was when she screwed Sery (and not only Sery) and people started thinking of her as his girlfriend. Sery probably didn't think so. But at least he didn't object.

They would meet and screw. Sometimes Svetka had the feeling that he loved her. "When you get a feeling about something, you should cross yourself," her grandmother used to say.

Sery didn't like Samson. He stank. Svetka agreed. The dog was a minor detail that wasn't worth arguing over.

Svetka didn't have any friends, only Yulka Mukhina from her year and Valya Kliueva from Magnitogorsk—they got to know each other by exchanging letters about how much they loved Leonardo DiCaprio. Although now they couldn't understand what it was they'd both liked about him.

At nine *Commissar Rex* started on the TV. Rex's master, Moser, looked a bit like Sery. Only Sery's head was shaved and Moser had hair.

Svetka felt thirsty. She drank plain boiled water with sugar. Samson stretched out on the doormat.

Svetka slept with Sery and thought about Oleg. Sery hung around with Oleg, so in a certain sense Sery was Oleg. Only partly, though. But he did hang out with him. It was crazy.

At a recent session Svetka had made friends with another part of Oleg—the drummer Anton. He'd turned up totally out of it, with his ear half ripped off. Sat down on the sofa and started drinking. He looked pitiful. He was sort of sickly anyway, sad. Rings in both his ears, in his nose and lip, in his nipples and navel. And that tattoo right across his back. Svetka liked him for that. But Anton had never let her near him—he never noticed girls. Except for Nastya.

But that night Anton couldn't give a shit and he was blind drunk. So was Svetka. She sat at his feet and unfastened his pants. At first Anton just sat there, sleeping. Then he looked down, amazed, probably thinking he was dreaming. An erotic dream . . .

Sery never found out. And if he had . . . well, he was "working two fronts" himself. Probably more than two. A major "star."

Ten o'clock. Svetka went to collect her books and notebooks for college. She hadn't dropped foreign literature. Fuck it anyway. Samson was yawning. Her student record book was lying under the bed. On the tube Nike Borzov was promising Svetka: *"I'm going to love you forever . . ."*

Eleven o'clock. Svetka left the house and walked to the bus stop. It was a long time before the bus came. Then when it came it was packed.

Twelve o'clock. Svetka was sitting in the hall reading about German romanticism. Oleg and Sery walked by.

"Hi!"

"Hi," said Svetka, biting her lip.

"Listen . . . I couldn't make it. Some other time."

"Yeah . . ."

"Never mind!" said Sery, more cheerfully. "How are you getting on?"

"Okay . . ."

"Great. How's Samson?"

"Samson's dead."

"Fantastic. Oleg and me have got to go. We'll take the exam tomorrow. I'll pick up your notes later, okay?"

Svetka nodded. She suddenly had the feeling she smelled of dog food. Sery smiled. Everything was fine.

7

In the evening Galya and Yulka went to the Dam. They'd finished all their exams, and even all their term papers. Returned all their books to the library. Handed in their student record books and library cards. They felt happy and blank. They didn't even feel like drinking. They just went to get a bit of air.

The sun flooded the walls of the houses with thick orange light and the air was filled with a heady smell of flowers and evening. There were horses at the Dam—50 rubles to experience the world of animals. Nervous girls with tanned legs tugged at the horses' reins every now and then, scaring off the drunks. The horses chewed on their bits and pissed on the pavement. Old women wandered around in the crowd, picking up empty bottles and sticking them in their bags. Dirty children competed with them.

There was a crowd standing in a semicircle beside the outdoor café. Galya and Yulka moved in closer.

"Same old water in the tap, same old broken chair . . ." sang a short little guy in a long shirt, rolling his startled eyes. He looked like Rolie Polie from the kids' cartoon. Beside him there was a drum kit, a synthesizer and two speakers. The bass guitarist was sitting on one of them with his legs dangling. A boy in a cap was standing behind the synthesizer, smoking as he played. The drummer was bald with glasses. Standing beside him and nodding his head in time, like a horse, the lead guitarist was wearing a Nirvana T-shirt. There was a fat saxophonist too, sitting on a chair. In front of him some half-drunk guys were dancing to the music.

"Fantastic," said Yulka.

"Fantastic," agreed Galya.

Everyone else there thought pretty much the same. Rolie Polie could sense it and he let himself go, wailing and growling into the microphone. The boy in the cap laughed as he backed him up—he couldn't have been more than fifteen. The fat saxophone player laughed too. The drummer's glasses glittered and he stuck his tongue out as he laid into the drums.

"They remind me of our own half-wits," said Yulka.

"Who?"

"Oleg and his band."

"Why, is that so bad?" Galya turned to her with a puzzled look.

"No, not at all. This is a gas, and Oleg's band is okay too . . ." Then she thought for a moment. "Naah, objectively speaking, Oleg's better . . ."

"Lie down, relax and listen to what I tell you," Rolie Polie began. The girls squealed. They forgave him for his poor voice because the music was good and it reminded them of things they loved.

"Calm down and shut your mouth." Galya repeated the song with just her lips. Yulka smiled at her.

They looked at the musicians. And then they saw. In a flash, like banging your head against a wall.

Yulka saw the bass guitarist. He was sitting there with a remote air, gazing straight ahead. He looked about twenty or twenty-five. Blue pants and sneakers. A crumpled T-shirt and blue hat. His face had an expression of tremendous, Olympian calm. It seemed as if, even if everything exploded and collapsed, he'd carry on sitting there, staring into space and nodding his head to the rhythm, fingering the strings. Yulka's mouth hung open, stupidly. Just at that moment the bass player looked at the drummer and smiled.

And Yulka was gone.

She was hooked on him instantly, after just one smile. But what a smile it was! It was the most tender, childlike, unpretentious smile Yulka had ever seen. Like in that Bon Jovi song: *"I will love you . . . A-a-a-always!"* Yulka was so far gone . . . she was insane, probably. She thought if only she were smiled at like that at the darkest moments of her life, then life would be simpler, life would be happier. Not so lousy after all.

Galya saw the boy wearing the cap. He was short, maybe up to Galya's shoulders. He had light-colored dreadlocks dangling from under the cap. A duck-billed nose and a wide mouth. What a delightful little piglet! thought Galya. And she wanted to touch him.

"Look!" said Yulka, nudging Galya with her elbow.

"What?" said Galya, coming back to reality.

"The bass player!" Yulka whispered in her ear in desperate delight. Galya eyed the bass player. A miserable, long kind of face, sitting there like he'd been smashed over the head.

"What about him?"

"Fantastic, isn't he?"

Galya scratched her nose and answered uncertainly, trying to avoid a conflict:

"Er . . . I don't know . . . The keyboard player's better."

Yulka looked at the keyboard player—a froglike creature too full of himself for his age.

"Nothing special . . ."

They said nothing for a while. Then Galya cautiously remarked:

"We've got different tastes, thank God."

"Yeah!" Yulka agreed immediately. It wasn't that the

bass player was no good; it was just that Galya's taste was . . . different.

They felt more cheerful now. Rolie Polie took the keyboard player's cap and went around collecting money. He looked at people with those startled eyes and they gave him ten rubles each time.

"I want to get to know them," said Galya.

"Me too."

"How?"

Yulka thought about it. She'd never gotten to know anyone just like that, in the street, but then she'd never met any bass players like that. The simplest thing would have been to go up and say something, but there were already four girls sitting beside the bass player, waiting to see if maybe he'd choose one of them. Yulka didn't want to be the fifth. Although five was her lucky number. Yulka looked at the bass player. He was staring into space, off in some dimension all his own. He didn't even notice Yulka or the other four.

At midnight the audience started to drift away, even though it was still light. The musicians were packing up, coiling up their cables. Galya had disappeared. Yulka was sitting on a stone parapet watching the water with her neck twisted around. It had grown cold. Suddenly Galya appeared out of nowhere, happy as a lark, with the keyboard player on her arm.

"Let me introduce you!" she yelled cheerfully. "This is Stasik!"

"Hello," said Stasik.

"Hi," said Yulka with a smile.

Stasik looked from her to Galya and back and thought: okay, let the good times roll, we've got fans. Galya laughed and gave Stasik a squeeze. They'd obviously had time to get a drink somewhere. It turned out that he was WildWildDen from the chat room. The girls who'd been less lucky and not managed to pick up a "star" were sitting on the stone steps nearby, watching Galya enviously.

"Stasik will introduce you to the bass player," Galya promised. "Right, Stas?"

"Sure . . . right now if you like."

"No need," said Yulka, afraid now, but it was too late— Galya grabbed her and dragged her into the crowd around the musicians. The bass player and the drummer were sitting drinking beer.

Stasik introduced them. "Max, Bob," he said, "this is Galya and . . ."

"Yulka," Galya prompted him.

"And Yulka."

The drummer held out his hand and the girls shook it in turn. Max looked at them, but there was still no reaction.

An hour later the entire band plus Yulka, Galya and another four girls (the ones who'd been waiting) were sitting in the Swineherd drinking. Yulka was sitting beside Max. He was smiling at all the girls in turn and drinking beer fifty-fifty with vodka.

"You shouldn't mix it like that," one of the girls, Elvira, said to him.

"I couldn't give a fuck."

He really couldn't give a fuck about anything.

Yulka sat there like an idiot, saying nothing. Galya got drunk and kissed Stasik. Bob the drummer found the sight really amusing.

Later, when they were all wasted, Max finally put his arm around Yulka. She trembled all over. This is unreal! she thought, feeling so happy she could choke. The bass player smiled. That same smile again. And it blew Yulka's mind.

"Let's go to my place," suggested Max.

"Okay," Yulka answered in a husky voice, not believing what was happening. She just couldn't grasp how it could happen like that—everything all at once in a single day. Concentrated essence of life.

She couldn't remember how they left the club, how they stopped a car, how they got upstairs to the fifth floor.

She came to on his sofa. He was sitting beside her and the TV was flickering, dull in front of them. They'd obviously only just gotten there. Max began to undress. He asked her:

"Why are you just sitting there?"

"What d'you mean?" asked Yulka, feeling scared.

"Get your clothes off."

"What for?"

He froze, amazed, then squatted down in front of Yulka.

"What did you come here for?"

"For you."

"Get your clothes off then!"

"What, are we going to fuck?" asked Yulka, feeling scared again.

"I said let's go to my place, and you agreed," Max said, emphasizing every word.

"I'd go anywhere you like with you, but I won't fuck you," Yulka said bluntly.

Max scratched his head. He'd obviously never found himself in such a stupid situation. He put his T-shirt back on and sat down beside her.

They sat there for a while. Max lit a cigarette. They

smoked one together. Two total strangers. Yulka was going insane. The bass player put on some music.

"I feel sleepy," said Yulka.

Max was totally bewildered now. But he started to make up a bed for her on the sofa. He stretched out on the floor. *"I wish I could be happy, I wish I wish I wish that something would happen . . ."* Yulka lay down too and closed her eyes. The bed was wide enough for three people to fit on it. The bass player looked at her.

"Lie down here," Yulka said to him in a hoarse voice. She was so crazy about him, she could have jumped off a roof: *"I will love you . . . always."*

He took off his T-shirt and settled in beside Yulka. Then she pulled him in under the blanket. He was confused now. He didn't know whether to come on to her or not. He asked:

"What's your name?"

"Yulka."

"Mine's Max."

"I know . . ."

"Where did a girl like you come from, Yulka?" the bass player asked, warily.

"I've always lived here. It's just that we never met before . . ."

"Thank God . . ."

"The way you play's fantastic," Yulka said cautiously, shivering inside. She'd come to someone else's house, and now she was lying on someone else's bed, annoying a stranger.

"Thanks," Max said with a grin. "What do you do?"

"I'm in college. Second year. Just finished."

"Are you eighteen?"

"Yeah. And you?"

"Twenty-three."

They said nothing for a while. They felt sleepy. The bass player yawned.

"Tell me about your band?" Yulka asked, struggling to keep her eyes open.

"It's a combination we put together," he said with a sleepy smile. "I'm in a different one as well . . ."

They soon fell asleep, pressed up close as if they were dearer to each other than anyone in the world and afraid of losing their way in life. That's always how it is when young people get drunk.

In the morning when Yulka woke up on the bass player's naked chest she couldn't believe it. She sat up on the divan and she still couldn't believe it. She refused to. The bass player was breathing steadily. Yulka gaped at him wide-eyed. She adored him. But she couldn't believe that it could happen like that. In a single day. Bang—everything all at once! Her parents would kill her when she got home. She got up quietly, took her handbag and left, trying not to make any noise. Afterward when she spoke about it she said she had absolutely no idea what she was doing. She just went home. She simply didn't believe in the concentrated essence of life.

Three days later Yulka and Galya went on another outing to the Dam. Yulka was so depressed that Galya had decided to give her brains an airing.

There was a crowd at the Dam. Rolie Polie & Co. were getting it on again.

Yulka spotted the bass player. He was sitting on a speaker, swinging his legs and nodding his head. Smiling, not reacting to a thing. Three girls with beer had installed themselves beside him. Another two were dancing. Yulka moved up into the front row. She stood there like a zombie. The bass player didn't see her. He looked at her and he didn't see her. Or maybe he didn't want to. Yulka stood there for a whole hour, while Rolie Polie sang ten songs and collected two capfuls of money. The bass player clowned around with the girls. The three with the beer.

Yulka turned around and walked away. She had this terrible feeling deep inside—like someone had torn a piece out of her soul. The bass player didn't want her. He had three others already . . . maybe even more. He took them home. And screwed them. Like he'd wanted to screw Yulka. Maybe she should have said yes?

Max watched Yulka leave. He had a feeling he'd seen her somewhere before. But he couldn't remember where.

8

The shadow of the branch swayed backward and forward on the ceiling. There was a smell of rain and cigarette smoke, not harsh, just in the background. Nastya watched the shadow on the ceiling. It felt as if the ceiling were sagging downward, making it harder for her to breathe . . . then easier again. The shadow swayed, looking like a hooked, childish hand . . . Nastya huddled down under the blanket, brushing against Steklov's warm shoulder. He was lying there breathing beside her and the ceiling wasn't falling in on him. Nastya sat up on the bed.

Yesterday they'd gone for a walk in the woods. Then they'd gone to the Youth Park and taken a ride on the roller coaster (Steklov had wanted to go on again, but Nastya's legs had turned to rubber and she was trembling), had some beer and then gone to Steklov's place "for tea" . . .

Nastya had always been unlucky with boys. Or rather, they'd always been unlucky with her. But she'd been unlucky too. She would fall in love with one (the strangest one—that was the best definition for her choice—not the handsome one, not the clever one, but the strange one), and he always happened to be the one who was already in love with her classmate or neighbor, girlfriend, film star, deeply and forever. Or maybe not in love, but busy anyway—with friends, work, heroin. Nastya simply couldn't figure out her own heart—or perhaps love isn't controlled by the heart after all, but by some cell in the brain, that's probably more likely—and she always picked "the wrong ones." There were other boys hanging around, not exactly a lot, but there were always some. Nastya wanted to love them, these available ones, so she wouldn't have to suffer. She once went on a date with one of them, Vova, a classmate. In tenth grade. Her girlfriends were already sleeping with boys; they boasted to each other about the positions they used and how their mothers would disapprove. But Nastya had never even been kissed. What a fool. She went with Vova to the nearest park. For a walk. It was obviously the first time Vova had been out with a girl too. He smoked nervously and swore more than usual.

They walked once around the pond and sat on a bench. Vova didn't speak. Neither did Nastya. Then he put his arm around her and tried to kiss her.

Nastya had felt so disgusted and sorry for herself that she wanted to cry. She had jumped up off the bench and ran out of the park, then wandered around the dark streets for hours, and when she got home she brushed her teeth thoroughly twice, even washed her mouth out with soap. That was the end of her experience with dates for a while.

So she got used to the idea that all her girlfriends paired up at the end of the night, wandering off in couples in the silence. She stayed at home instead and read books. And anyway she was fascinated by astronomy. She and her friend Liudka Kolosova watched the stars through a telescope. Then afterward the two of them drew the constellations in a notebook. Liudka was unlucky with boys too—she was plump and she had a terrible complex about it. Nastya wasn't plump. She was slim, impetuous and embarrassed about her appearance. For no apparent reason.

There was no tea at Steklov's place, so they drank a little gin and wine. But there was a bucket of wild strawberries collected by Steklov and his mother the day before. Nastya drank, ate and went out of her mind. Then they moved from the kitchen into the room. Pashka put on *The Truman Show* with Jim Carrey. Not really the best film to create an intimate setting, but ten minutes later Nastya and Steklov were kissing. He pulled off her skirt and panties, unzipped his own fly and they screwed without getting undressed. Then they folded out the sofa bed, got undressed and carried on.

* * *

When she first went to college, Nastya had no plans to make any romantic connections—she'd gotten used to the idea that she'd never have anyone. Well, not that she'd never have anyone, but not right now, perhaps in a year or two. It was depressing, of course—but otherwise she'd have had to tear that cell out of her brain. Only how?

Nastya sat in the front row in class, took down notes on the lecture, revised them at home; she'd already gotten three A's in Russian and written a term paper before she got to know Anton.

Their group was taking the history exam; the lecturer believed that the more time she took to test their knowledge as thoroughly as possible, the better it was for everyone. The line stretched right down the hall. Nastya had been working in the library and was one of the last to arrive. So now she was stuck there until seven o'clock, waiting to take the test. Not on her own, of course. Lyokha Petrov, Kostya Patrushev, Yulka Mukhina and Anton were all still there at the end. They hardly knew each other, but now they became friends. Lyokha told them about all sorts of horrors that were supposedly in store for students during the first exam session. Kostya was genuinely scared and Yulka laughed nervously and tried to make a joke of it, and then she told them how last summer she'd gone to the country and almost drowned. Nastya had been inspired by the spirit of universal love and friendship in their year. They'd inspected Anton's piercings—three holes in each ear, one in his nose and one in his eyebrow.

Yulka had gone through to take the test, followed by Kostya and Lyokha. Then it was Anton's turn. Nastya was last in line and she couldn't care less anymore how she did.

She was really hungry. The darkness outside was a dense shade of blue. It was cold.

Anton came out and she went in, holding her notes out in front of her. The history lecturer was smoking and staring at the wall. She didn't even turn to look at Nastya. Eventually she took Nastya's notes and asked her a couple of questions about dates. The lecturer had thick clumps of coarse little black hairs on her upper lip. She looked like a tormented spaniel.

Finally Nastya emerged with a sigh of relief. The empty corridor was silent. Anton squatted against the wall. When he saw Nastya he got up quickly.

"What are you doing here?" she asked in surprise.

"Waiting for you," said Anton in a voice that sounded strange, guilty. "It's late, after all."

Nastya hadn't expected that. Anton stuck his hands in his pockets and walked beside her. They went downstairs and Nastya put her jacket on while Anton said nothing, looking off to one side. At the bus stop he asked her:

"Where are you going to?"

"Decembrist Square."

They stood there for half an hour, and then Anton suggested:

"Let's walk. I'll see you home."

"Okay," Nastya agreed.

They walked side by side without speaking. After a while Nastya asked him the only question she could think of:

"How many points did you get?"

"Fourteen. And you?"

"Fifteen."

"Well done!" said Anton happily. Quite sincerely, as if Nastya were his daughter or maybe even his sister.

"You too!"

They laughed.

"So what are you into in general?"

"I . . . er . . . play music . . ." said Anton, embarrassed. "I play percussion, and piano . . ."

Later Nastya discovered that music went along with piercing, tattoos and grass. Or heroin on special days. Sometimes all of them together at the same time, with beer or vodka. Anton and his friends got drunk, smoked grass, then someone would shoot up and they'd use the same needle to pierce another hole in Anton's ear. And not only Anton's, of course. Then Gesha, a master tattoo artist, would get involved. A great life, really. Lots of fun.

Steklov was sweaty and sticky. He went to get washed and then lay down beside Nastya. Kissed her and said "Good night."

Nastya didn't like Anton to shoot up, so he gave up heroin. He didn't think hash was anything serious. But when Nastya asked to try it, he frowned and said:

"Just stay away from all that shit, all right? It's not for you . . . I don't want you to be like them . . ."

He meant his own friends.

But more and more Anton neglected his friends (they understood him and didn't take offense—for Anton, that was the way real friends acted), and he skipped the hash and music in order to spend some time with Nastya. To sit beside her while she talked about her constellations. To drink tea with her and Liudka Kolosova. Then to be left alone with her. To sit there hugging Nastya, like two little animals in their burrow. Feeling warm. With someone special. They didn't even kiss. They just talked.

Then Nastya kissed him herself. It wasn't disgusting, quite the opposite. And then they slept together for the first time. At Anton's place. After, Anton sat on the windowsill in nothing but his jeans, smoking. Nastya drank coffee. Then she looked at him.

"You know, I've never seen you so happy," she said in surprise.

Anton sighed, unable to describe the feeling that filled his heart, or rather that cell in his brain. He whispered:

"I've never been so happy . . ."

And then, frightened that Nastya would get the wrong idea, he explained hastily:

"It's not the sex, honestly. Or not just that . . . I . . . I'd die without you."

"Me too."

Nastya met Steklov in her second year. They stood beside each other in the library. Then they ran into each other in the cafeteria. Steklov was in fourth year. He was already working as a manager somewhere, but his personality was more like a schoolboy's. He was a little thick, really. But good-looking. And what was most important, all Nastya's friends liked him, apart from Liudka Kolosova. They didn't like Anton. Too many things about him were "all wrong." He dressed all wrong, he spoke all wrong, he came home late and disappeared for weeks at a time. Nastya listened to all this from her friends and the other girls in her year, and she tried to change their minds, but they ended up changing hers. But with Steklov, there were no problems.

"Steklov's so cool!" the girls said enviously, and Nastya was thrilled.

She started neglecting Anton.

Steklov didn't smoke, he didn't get high, he didn't booze in the clubs and he didn't lie around on the floor totally out of it. Of course, Anton wrote songs. About Nastya. But Steklov knew how to say the right things. It was all so easy with him.

A week ago Nastya had officially finished it with Anton. She felt bad about it, but not that bad. Changes were always stressful. Like those first nights at summer camp. Nastya used to cry into her pillow, but then the homesickness would pass and she spent days on end happily fooling around with other children. You can get used to anything.

The shadow of the branch faded. Then suddenly it was outlined sharply in the bright beam from a late car's headlights. Brakes squealing, the car drove away, rustling over the road. The cool silence returned.

Nastya lay there trying to understand why she felt so terrible. She tried to convince herself it was nothing but "echoes of the past," that it would soon pass. Like at summer camp when she was younger.

But then she realized it wasn't going to pass.

* * *

Yesterday Liudka had told her:

"You're a fool. Why do you let other people decide everything for you?"

"Ha! Not true!" Nastya had retorted. "I do everything the way I want to."

"Ha!" Liudka came right back. "Like what, for instance?"

Nastya realized the conversation would gradually get around to personalities and Liudka would start drilling into her head what a bad person she was for dumping Anton. She said:

"I chose Steklov myself. So you can keep your nose out of it."

"No you didn't. They chose him for you, you stupid fool. Those so-called friends of yours, who couldn't give a shit . . ."

She left without finishing the sentence . . .

9

Sashka Berdyshev was celebrating his "final June" drinking on his own in the kitchen. It all flew past in front of his eyes—shadows, garbage, thoughts—building up into a story without any beginning—to be continued. The beginning was somewhere in the past, but he hadn't bothered to think then what it was all for. Sashka was drinking, but not to "get drunk"; it was to show "all of them." But who "they" were he didn't really know. He'd invented them all as shadows and garbage, and he shouted at them. There were some he loved. And he'd always thought of himself as fortunate. If it was there in your brains, then it was real. That meant you could tell real people about it. Or live your life in that world, lock yourself away in there, not let them in. Not anyone. Even your best friend. His friend was lucky; he had everything and more to spare. Sashka had the thoughts, shadows and garbage he'd used to construct his own life story. He'd never let anyone in on it, it didn't exist, it was somewhere else, not here. He'd forgotten about it and only remembered yesterday, when there was no one to screw. Sashka was just drinking and thinking about nothing; there were things he wanted and things he dreamed about, but only inside, in silence. He'd always said, kind of in passing, that he had a girl somewhere. Curiosity or questions were just totally shattered. But he said nothing, and everyone thought he was saying it about something. But he was just saying nothing because he wasn't living. Or maybe he was living, only not here. Maybe he even loved someone. Only not them.

His friends inspired him to great things. He played the clubs instead of Sery, standing there staring at the floor. He didn't know the songs. He had his own.

He got up, lit a cigarette, looked out of the window. There were people's shadows out there, and garbage from the dump flying around. The clouds covered the sky with patterns of dots and squares, he thought. He knew he was only a visitor, that someday he'd go back to where he was born. He'd leave his friend behind, but his friend would forget. And there was no one else; he had them all with him. Even naked in the bath he talked to them. Laughed, joked and wept, sobbing violently. He didn't want anybody, they were all in the past. Maybe not even in the past, but not there. Everyone he needed had bought a ticket and left ages ago. Maybe at lunchtime. While Sashka was sleeping.

He stubbed his cigarette out against the wall and took another. There was something bothering him; he couldn't figure out what. He wanted to be real and feel where he was. So he could put his arms round someone. Make love, and then not think he was alone and he'd invented it all. He loved real people, but as if they were in a zoo. They sat in the cages and he wandered around. Sometimes he threw them a piece of himself, and they watched without understanding. They said: "I love you," and he answered: "I don't need that."

Sashka drank four shots of gin, then opened some beer. He drank with a grimace, thinking about the meaning of life lying in his pocket. Idiot. Yesterday he'd opened all the doors and windows and the rain had burst into the house like a ticket to wherever. Sashka had jumped around like a little kid, singing songs. The neighbors downstairs had banged on the ceiling to get him to stop. That had made him furious and he'd put Metallica on at full blast. They'd hammered on the door, but he hadn't opened it. The phone had rung. It was a familiar voice. It asked what was going on. He said he was drinking. He didn't know anything, didn't remember anything. It was easier to live like that, but it made it harder for the others. He'd promised to go to the Swineherd yesterday. But he hadn't gone, and he'd let down his friends and his girlfriend. She called and breathed into the receiver. He'd understood and put the phone down. She'd called again; he'd gone out for a minute. And not come back for an hour.

He came back and waited; she didn't call. She'd given up on him, reluctantly. He thought she was just sleeping; she wasn't sleeping. He was smiling and flying away. Far away. There was a knock on the door. He opened it. Saw them standing there. His real friends. He said:

"Hi."

They answered gloomily:

"Hi."

He loved them all so much his heart hurt. He couldn't breathe when they weren't there, so he smoked. And in his brain he invented a little door out of the shadows, so he'd always be in the center and always love them.

Oleg asked:

"Why didn't you come yesterday?"

"I was drinking," Sashka said with a shrug.

"Tsk-tsk . . ." said Sery with a frown. He went through into the kitchen and downed the rest of the beer in a single swig.

Oleg took a guitar and sank onto the sofa. He sang: *"I'm just gonna die!"* Sashka laughed. Probably from happiness. That he wasn't alone. The phone rang.

She said:

"I'll be there at ten . . ."

In an icy voice, so he wouldn't get any ideas. Sashka understood. He pressed the phone against his ear and whispered so they wouldn't hear:

"I'm sorry . . ."

She smiled wearily into the phone and put it down. He felt the beeps in his hand. Sashka stood there. He was happy. Oleg started singing: *"Without you I'm just gonna die . . ."*

"D'you know this one?"

I don't know how to hold you, when you want . . .
I'm simply going to die,
Stay here with me,
Here at my side, though I spoil everything,
For you I'll try . . .

Sashka took another guitar and began to play along. Sery yelled at him to stop missing the notes. Sashka told him to go to hell. They swore at each other for a long time, but only joking, not for real.

Outside the cold sun was rising; the trams were coming to life and clanging on the rails. Oleg was sleeping, Sery was smoking, Sashka woke up and saw shadows. Garbage flying through the air, blocking his eyes. There was someone breathing beside him. Oleg. After the Sphinx club. The doorbell rang, he went to open up. She was standing on the doorstep—real and in the flesh.

She smiled through her hurt.

"Hi, Sashka."

"Hi," was what he was going to say. He changed his mind in an instant, just hugged her and stuck his face into her shoulder, barely alive. She stood there up to her neck in tender feelings, choking, thinking: It's time to finish this. Sashka was two years younger—it was ridiculous. But she loved him. She really loved him. And she could probably manage to forgive him.

10

The smoke in the flat was so thick it made their eyes water. Yulka and Oleg were sitting in the kitchen. Drinking beer. Outside the window the cool leaves were rustling, and some dog was barking. Nonstop, on and on, like clockwork. The barking mingled with the night air and came in through the open small window. Forcing the cigarette smoke back.

"How's life?" asked Oleg.

"Fine," said Yulka, listening to herself. She realized that actually it was lousy. Oleg realized it too.

"Everything will be okay," he promised her uncertainly.

"Yeah . . ." Yulka didn't believe him. "Some fine day on Thursday."

"Yes, why not on Thursday . . ."

They glanced at the tear-off calendar. "Eighteenth of January, Tuesday."

"Nothing's going to happen at that kind of speed," Yulka complained miserably. She tried to disguise her tone of voice with a grin, but it came out sounding sour.

Oleg took a swig, put the bottle down and picked up a guitar.

"Play your song," Yulka said.

Oleg nodded with a smile and started playing the melody. He sang, not straining his voice, like at a gig, but quietly:

You waited for me, but you got too tired,
I tried to catch the moments, hold them in my hand,
You gave up and you left just for a while
But now you don't want to come back again . . .

He looked straight into Yulka's eyes and said:

You screwed someone, I'm ready to forgive,
You kissed someone not me, but what,
What did you think, as you lay on his chest?
You told me that I spoil your life, spoil everything . . .

Yulka shivered. Oleg seemed to come to his senses.

"Sorry . . ."

She was silent. Oleg lit up and looked out the dark window. The windowsills hadn't cooled off yet. Steam was rising from the ground; there was a smell of dense foliage. And cut grass. The regular "woof-woof-woof" was like the ticking of a clock. The bluish smoke dissolved into the air, Oleg blew it off to one side, screwing his eyes up. Yulka looked at his golden curls. By the light of the bare bulb hanging from the ceiling, they looked ash-gray.

Masha Nikonova and Kostya Patrushev came bursting into the kitchen. Kostya was already staggering, but for some reason Masha was sober. Very strange. Everyone else had gotten wasted . . .

"How's that Steklov of yours doing?" asked Yulka.

Masha gave her a look, then held up her middle finger in reply. Yulka wasn't bothered. Masha poured some water into a glass from a pitcher and went out, taking Kostya with her.

Nobody said anything for a while. Oleg stubbed his cigarette out on a bottle and flicked the butt out the window. Then he picked up the guitar. Started to play.

"'A Song for the Lovers,'" said Yulka, recognizing it. "You've learned it?"

"Yeah," said Oleg with a smile. "And I got the text off the Net . . . But it's a waste of time."

"Why is it?"

Oleg looked at Yulka.

"I ought to be writing my own stuff, not doing this . . ."

"You do write."

Oleg shrugged. Smiled. Repeated in a detached voice, syllable by syllable:

"A waste of time . . ."

"Why?"

Oleg looked at Yulka and put the guitar down. Svetka came into the kitchen. Made a show of sitting down on the windowsill. Lit a cigarette and twisted it in her fingers. Yulka began feeling uncomfortable. Awkward. Oleg picked up a beer.

In the room The Backstreet Boys were blasting away:

"Tell me why I can't be there where you are . . ." The bass player Seryoga was yelling, trying to shout over them: *"I can't do a thing about it, I can't change a thing, there's nothing left for me to do—I'm going to live!"*

"You've pissed me off, you and your Dolphin," yelled Galya Romanova, tearing herself away from the drunken lips of Lyokha Petrov.

"You shut up!" Sery retorted cheerfully and carried on even louder than before: *"No matter what anyone says—I'm going to live!"*

"Drop dead, will you!" Galya said.

Sashka laughed. He began jumping up and down with Seryoga and yelling:

"A party at the children's home, all the local guys and dolls are shooting up."

"Let's put together a band," suggested Sery.

Marinka was sleeping on the sofa, oblivious to the music and all the other noise. She was blind drunk. Anton was lying beside her. Staring up blankly at the ceiling.

Kostya Patrushev and Liudka Kolosova were screwing on the balcony. Not for any apparent reason. But they were out of it too.

The doorbell rang. Yulka went to answer it. Svetka grinned as she watched her go. She looked at Oleg. He noticed the grin, guessed correctly what the look meant and said in a quiet voice:

"Svet . . . Don't waste your time on me . . ."

"Waste it?" Svetka didn't understand.

Oleg bit his lip and nodded. Then for some reason he added:

"Everything will be just fine . . . *I play a song for the lovers . . ."*

"What?"

Nastya walked through into the room and looked around. Everyone was swimming in cigarette smoke, dancing. Lying in the corners. She went into the kitchen, saw Oleg and Svetka Ryabova there. Oleg smiled. Svetka was sitting with her forehead pressed against the glass. She didn't want them to see her crying. It wasn't like there was any real reason.

Nastya went out into the hall and sat on the dressing table with her head in her hands. She heard someone walk over and stand beside her. She looked up and her lashes were wet.

"I knew you'd come . . ." said Anton.

"How?"

He looked at her and his eyes were red.

"Because you love me." Then he bit his pale lips and added: "No matter what anyone says . . ."

vasya and the
green men

the green men only turned up here fairly recently. They hung out near the garbage dump, fishing the scraps of food out of old tin cans. Eating potato peelings. The green men were very fond of potato peelings. Especially if they were mixed up with broken eggshells—that was how their bodies got calcium. They didn't much like chewing chalk, though I don't really know why. During the day they sat behind the trash heaps and fought each other over every morsel of food. The green men were quite a bit bigger than the local bums and they used to take their bottles away from them. They used to take bums in there behind the heaps and beat them. Kick them and punch them and hit them with bottles. On the head. The bums groaned and tore at the green men with their long dirty nails. Sometimes they scratched their legs and made them bleed. But not many bums managed to escape from the green men. They tore the bums to pieces, gouged out their eyes and ate them. And then they licked the wounds on their legs. The green men had long, thick, purple tongues. With saliva constantly dripping from them. That was where the puddles behind the trash heaps came from. It was the green men's saliva running and collecting into pools.

The green men couldn't talk. They could only growl and bellow or snort like horses. They snorted a lot, so the trash heaps were all slimy because their snot stuck to them.

At night the green men came out from behind the heaps, took a look around, and then made a dash to hide in the alleyways between the houses to get warm. You could often see a cluster of little red lights by the radiator—that was the venomous gleam of the green men's eyes. And once they got warm, the green men used to climb up the walls of the houses to the balconies and cut out the windowpanes with their sharp nails. Then they ate jam and pickled tomatoes, cucumbers and potted plants.

In spring the green men went wild. They gnawed the rust off the Dumpsters, growling and whining. They found it hard even to move, and they couldn't piss at all, so they puked. They smelled particularly repulsive in spring. What they wanted were vagrant women. They used to drag the women behind the trash heaps and rape them with their long purple tongues and their thick purple pricks that were just as long. Sometimes for weeks at a time, panting and growling. The women died, of course. To make sure no traces were left, the green men dismembered them and ate them. Who cares what happens to vagrants anyway?

But the green men couldn't get hold of these women very

often, so they used to catch ordinary old women instead. They smelled of rotten onions and old woman's sweat, but the green men didn't care. They raped the old women regardless, shredding their wrinkled bodies to pieces with their dirty nails. Then they licked their nails and sucked the blood and bits of guts out from under them.

If it weren't for Vasya, these green men would have carried on living like this, and no one would ever have known about them. Vasya was a short, puny little kid who lived near the dump. Because he was so puny he wore his father's old oversized pants. Sticking up out of them were the red underpants his mother had sewn for him out of a Nazi flag. The flag used to belong to Vasya's brother Fedya, who shaved his head and went around in his father's boots (which he'd modernized by putting in red laces through holes he made with a spike). But Fedya had disappeared six months ago, and his mother had decided to put his flag to good use. Vasya had also inherited his tattered shirts from his father's shoulders, and even his watch. It was old and broken, but it had a long chain. Vasya attached it to his pants and the chain dangled out of his pocket. Everyone laughed at Vasya for that and beat him. They beat him on his head, his stomach and in the teeth. So it was a good thing Vasya was still young and he only had his baby teeth.

All right then. It all started one fine day, or rather, night, when Vasya was sitting in his room (actually it was Fedya's room, but Fedya wasn't there, so Vasya had been moved into it) and crying. Vasya's cute little face was all puffed up and painful, and all because the kids in the street had laughed at Vasya's wide pants, which Vasya's dad had already worn through when they belonged to him. Vasya had taken offense and told the other kids to fuck off. The other kids had taken offense too and they'd given Vasya a vicious beating over the head with bricks, plus they'd smashed in his front teeth with an iron pipe.

When Vasya came crawling home, his mother swore at him, his granddad spat on him, and his father chipped in with a beating around the ear with his slipper. And now Vasya was crying as he pressed the phone against his swollen ear.

"I'm licking it, rhythmically tightening and relaxing my grip . . ." the voice in the phone intoned languidly. But even that wasn't enough to lift Vasya's spirits. Then suddenly his gaze was drawn to the window. Something green and man-shaped went running across the roof of the shop across the street. Then the green thing dashed across to a balcony, scrambled rapidly up onto it and disappeared. Vasya stopped crying, puzzled.

A thought flashed through his battered brain. What's that? Vasya took his hand out of his Nazi underwear and scratched his head. Then he put the phone back on the hook and scratched his bruised head again, which made his bumps and bruises start hurting even worse. Vasya whined quietly, but carried on thinking: What was that fucker? Where'd it come from? And how come it runs so fast? But alas, no answers to all his questions turned up. So Vasya went to bed.

Like all children, Vasya went to school. So that was where he went when he woke up the next morning. At school everyone laughed at Vasya because he had no front teeth. The sixth-year boys even tried to fuck with him in the bathroom, but they couldn't get his mouth open.

After school Vasya went home, the same as always. He got into the elevator and pressed the button for the ninth floor. As he rode up he was wondering what to do about his teeth: maybe he should get his granddad's. His granddad was going to die soon anyway—he didn't really need his teeth, but they'd do fine for Vasya . . . then suddenly the elevator got stuck. "Shit!" said Vasya to himself and he pressed the "Call Help" button. The speaker gave a hoarse wheeze and he heard a brief snatch of speech: "I'm licking it, rhythmically tightening and relaxing my grip . . ." Vasya felt like he was cut off from the world. A child abandoned and all alone. He was about to burst into tears.

Suddenly he heard a vile gurgling sound behind him and smelt an abominable stench. Do I really smell that bad? wondered Vasya. It's not surprising, I suppose. I never wash, do I? My underpants are practically glued on . . . Vasya spent a few moments engrossed in these reflections before he decided to turn his head.

There was a huge man standing in the corner of the elevator, dressed in green rags. He was rolling his eyeballs and glaring maliciously, and he had yellow pus running out from under his eyelids and bunches of coarse hairs sticking out of his nostrils. He was clacking his teeth like castanets and his purple-gray tongue was dangling down onto his chest. For a second Vasya tried to figure out what kind of ugly fucker this was. Then the next second, one of the green man's sweaty, stinking hands grabbed Vasya by the neck and the other plunged its flaking nails into his left eye and tugged it out. Blood and slime ran down Vasya's cheek and his veins snapped with a crunch.

Vasya came to beside the trash chute on the fifth floor. His hair was matted with blood and stuck to the floor. Vasya fearfully felt himself all over. When he got to his left eye, it was still there. But for some reason he couldn't see very well—everything was kind of dim and murky. At home he looked in the mirror. His face was all covered in blood, and instead of his eye there was something white, with a pink stamp on it. A table-tennis ball . . .

Vasya didn't sleep a wink all night. He just lay there thinking: Fucking hell! The cold spring wind howled rhythmically outside his window and Vasya's thoughts surged to the same rhythm in his head. Suddenly he heard a stealthy scraping sound above the howling—as though someone were scratching a stone along the windowsill outside. Vasya raised his head, then instantly huddled back down under the blanket, almost pissing his pants in fear. There were two red eyes staring in at him out of the darkness. The eyes blinked and disappeared. Vasya dashed over to the window and looked down and saw a shadowy figure zigzagging rapidly across the yard. It ran behind the shop and disappeared. Spooks . . . thought Vasya. Holy shit!

The next day the other kids on the street beat Vasya up again. They didn't like the way he ogled them with his plastic eye. Lena Sakharova even called Vasya an obscene name. Anyway, Vasya came home really upset, with his pants torn. His mother smacked him on the head with the meat grinder for the ruined pants and sent him to the shop to get some bread. His father was up in arms too, brandishing the telephone bill. But the kids in the yard took Vasya's money and plastic bag and they wanted to take his watch and chain as well, only Vasya wouldn't let them. So for that they drove him up onto the roof of the boiler house and took away the ladder. Okay, thought Vasya. I'll get you back someday. Then he lay down on the roof and went to sleep.

He was awoken by strange noises and when he looked down out of the window, again he almost pissed his pants.

Old Granny Anya was lying down there like a little corpse on the open space in front of the dump, with a crowd of green men jostling around her and tearing at her with their dirty nails, licking and biting and even raping her, although she was obviously a goner already. They were all wheezing and panting greedily. The spittle and blood were running together into puddles and some of the green men were licking it all up and choking on it. Suddenly Vasya spotted the one he knew—dressed in rags, with his eyes rolling and his tongue lolling out. He tore out the old woman's eye, popped it into his mouth and chewed on it gloomily. Why, the fuckers! thought Vasya.

The men ate the guts out of Granny Anya's belly and bit off her fingers and toes. One of them had torn her nose off and was sucking on it. Holy shit! thought Vasya.

Vasya was annoyed that his own eye had been gobbled up just like that. The table-tennis ball was pretty good too, of course, but an eye was more useful. I've got to do something! thought Vasya, and with his third thought he fell asleep from all the strain.

In the morning, after he'd turned things over in his little brain, Vasya came to the conclusion that it was no good throwing himself on the green men with his penknife; the blade was blunt anyway. What if the green men didn't get the idea and just gobbled Vasya up, complete with all his youthful giblets and his tiny brain? And then sucked on his nose as well, the big ugly bastards. I'll have to ask the grown-ups for advice! thought Vasya.

His father's nerves were bad—he didn't understand that the green men had eaten Granny Anya at the dump. He gave Vasya a good smacking upside the head with his slipper, and then spat on him in annoyance.

Vasya sobbed as he scraped off his dad's spittle, still wondering what to do.

But next day there was a surprise waiting for Vasya—his grandpa had died, leaving his grandson his false teeth and a bottle of fox poison as his inheritance. Vasya's granddad had once successfully used the poison on Vasya's grandmother (but no one had guessed). He'd also used it on several occasions to get rid of neighbors' dogs, but not all of them, only the ones that bit. Oh, Vasya's granddad had been up to all sorts of things with that poison of his. Too many things to remember them all, but even Vasya's badly battered little brain immediately realized this was something he could find a use for.

That night he dragged granddad and his coffin out onto the staircase landing and loaded them into the elevator.

His mother and father were blind drunk (on account of their sudden stroke of luck), so they didn't hear the scraping and banging. Holy shit! Vasya thought in delight. In the elevator he smeared his granddad thoroughly all over with fox poison and then poured poison into his eyes, nose (which was difficult) and mouth. He daubed granddad's hair and parted it neatly. The lift squeaked as it set off downward and Vasya's courage sank at the same rate. Even the glass of vodka he'd downed on the sly wasn't any help.

Vasya's watch chain jangled as he dragged the coffin out into the street. Then he moved it over to the garbage dump, set it down and splashed over a bit more poison. He ran off into the bushes and pulled up his pants, which were slipping down. An hour later the green men started arriving at the dump. They were feeling mean and hungry, because that day they hadn't caught a single bum or vagrant woman, or even an old woman. They were starving and the saliva was dripping off their purple tongues, leaving a trail along the asphalt. So it wasn't surprising that when they saw the corpse, they flung themselves on it, growling and biting. Every one of them tried to grab the biggest chunk he could. They crunched up the gristle and the guts, chewing on the nose and ears, ripping the eyes out with their dirty, stinking nails. Vasya wanted to puke, but he thought he'd probably better leave that for some other time. Just in case they still weren't full after they finished eating granddad . . .

Half an hour later the space in front of the dump was strewn with the stinking corpses of the green men. They lay there with their eyes bulging out and their tongues swollen and black. Pus was bubbling out of their nostrils in streams of yellow foam. Vasya was puking in the bushes.

Then suddenly Vasya's nose twitched at a familiar smell! He looked around and saw the massive ugly fucker with festering red eyes coming straight at him with his clawed hands clenched into fists.

So Vasya booked it—what else could he do?

The chain banged against Vasya's leg, his father's pants slipped down onto his hips, making it hard to run, and with only one eye Vasya couldn't see too well. But he ran anyway, with his little pink tongue hanging out, choking on his own snot.

The green man was gaining on him fast when suddenly the ground went out from under Vasya's feet. He went hurtling downward and landed heavily on something foul-smelling and soft. He sprang to his feet in what appeared to be a well. The moon was shining into the darkness and on the bottom, right under his feet, Vasya saw a decayed corpse with grinning teeth and empty eye sockets. Vasya might confuse the letters of the alphabet and not remember phone numbers too well, but he recognized those boots right away—with the red laces in the holes punched with a spike. Fe-edya! he thought despairingly. But he didn't call out. He could hear gurgling sounds and stamping feet right above his head, so he decided to lie low.

There was a bellow that was repeated several times, and then everything went quiet. Vasya sighed in relief (because he'd taken a piss in the well) and started climbing out. The yard was empty. Vasya cautiously sat down on a bench; then suddenly everything started going hazy and he saw bright green circles spinning in front of his one eye. His brain started spinning slowly too, and he felt like he wanted to puke. Vasya blacked out.

The next day the kids beat Vasya up again for lying on the bench where he shouldn't have been and for stinking so badly. His mother got a smack in too: "Where've you been you fucker," she said, "your granddad's disappeared!" And when his father heard the story about the green man he stubbed his cigarette out on Vasya's tongue. So he wouldn't talk such stupid shit.

The dead green men were eaten up by the local dogs (and a few of the pensioners, but we won't name any names). The well was filled in with concrete, sealing Fedya's bones inside.

So now there are bums all over the place again, and the old women can take their garbage out after nine o'clock at night. And no one in the town could ever have imagined it all happened thanks to the puny ten-year-old kid Vasya—in his father's oversized pants with his Nazi underwear sticking up out of them and the chain from his father's broken watch dangling down at one side, in a torn checkered shirt that also used to be his father's, with his front teeth smashed out and a celluloid table-tennis ball instead of one eye. With his badly battered head shaved short (because of lice). And when they see Vasya, no one thinks: Here comes a hero! For some reason everyone thinks, Who's this ugly fucker? and the kids on the street beat Vasya even harder and even stick needles under his fingernails. But Vasya couldn't give a shit about them; he just comes home and sits all night with the phone pressed up against his ear, listening to the tired voice saying: "I'm licking it, rhythmically tightening and relaxing my grip . . ."

remote feelings

h e's impossible to love," said Nastya, cracking a sunflower seed between her teeth.

"He's impossible not to love," Mashka said, contradicting her.

"No, he's impossible to love," Nastya repeated calmly. "He's impossible not to love, but he's impossible to love."

"Why?"

"There's no point. It's like looking at a poster of some band you love. Only worse."

"How so worse?"

"They're not real. They're nothing but a picture. But he's alive, standing right there beside you—you could just reach out and touch him. He's accessible, but he's not accessible. It would ruin your entire life."

"That's a little much!" Mashka objected. "Not my entire life, maybe a week of it at most."

"That's just what you think," chuckled Nastya, staring into space.

Nastya was in second year and she knew everything. Sablin was a womanizer and a poser. Mashka was a naïve first-year student. The two didn't fit together.

Mashka went out into the hall. Sablin was standing in front of the bulletin board with the schedule. Curly hair, crumpled sweatshirt, sloppy jeans, thick-soled shoes. But that was okay. The clothes only concealed his body; they didn't become part of it. Some guys pulled on a shirt or jacket and they looked as if they'd been born in that kind of gear. But even bad clothes wouldn't have spoiled Sablin.

He stood there for a while and then went into the lecture hall, handsome and pleasant. Zero attention for Mashka. No time for her. They were on different planets! The slob. The conceited idiot.

Mashka sat back down at the desk and thought for a moment. Then she tore a page out of her notebook, and, trying not to use her own handwriting, she traced out the words: "Hello, bright sun. Please rise earlier and come to class more often. It's dark and sad here without you." She thought for another moment and signed it: "M.N." Then she folded the page up and wrote on it: "L. Sablin, Third Year."

Now all she had to do was pin the note to the bulletin board. Mashka came out into the hall and looked around.

There were plenty of people about, but Sablin wasn't there. She went over to the bulletin board and carefully looked over all the announcements. Then she plucked off a pushpin, used it to put up her note and stared at the notices. She wasn't doing anything. Just reading the notices. But the blood was pounding in Mashka's temples as if she'd just run two laps of the park in P.E.

The next morning the weather was incredibly lovely. The sun wasn't fully up yet, but it was already warming the air when Mashka pulled open the heavy door with the carved wooden handle and plunged into the stone coolness of the university.

Mashka went up to the fourth floor, nodded to her class-mate Kraev and said hello to Nastya. She walked past the bulletin board, glancing at all the different bits of paper out of the corner of her eye and then froze on the spot . . .

There was a note hanging on the timetable: "M.N. from A.S."

Mashka tore the note off with trembling hands and un-folded it.

"Hello! I'm sorry, I must be an idiot, but I didn't under-stand what the initials 'M.N.' mean. Today (4/27) I actually managed to get up at 7:40, but I had to go somewhere else. I'm sorry. Write me something nice . . ."

Mashka stood there as if she'd been hit over the head. The words sank in bit by bit. First "hello," then the exclama-tion mark . . . Mashka glanced around. What if Sablin hap-pened to be standing somewhere nearby? She'd just grabbed it, without thinking . . . So much for all her caution! Idiot . . .

Nastya came over. Looked closely at Mashka.

"What's up?"

"Nothing . . ." Mashka's cheeks blazed bright red.

"What's that in your hand?"

"A note," Mashka whispered jubilantly. She was positively oozing happiness and wanted to share it with someone. She handed the sheet of paper to Nastya.

"A.S." Nastya read out in a loud voice, and then translated. "Alexander Sablin. Lyosha . . . Yep . . . 'seven-forty . . . something nice . . .'"

She handed the note back.

"It's a load of crap. He's got you confused with someone else."

Mashka didn't want to believe that. Sablin was a nice guy. Otherwise why would he write "I'm sorry" and "write me something nice"?

"You're not in school anymore. He's just being polite." Nastya cracked a sunflower seed between her teeth and spat the husk out into her hand.

"He smiled at me once," Mashka suddenly remembered. "In the hall. And afterward, when he looked back into the hall . . ."

"You're not in school anymore," Nastya repeated, cracking another sunflower seed. "He's a grown man. You ogle him, and he smiles back. Out of politeness. Or because he feels like a star. And like you're one of his fans."

Mashka was horrified.

"Do you think he knows?"

"No, probably not. He's just polite."

A girl from the third year went up to the bulletin board. Short hair, glasses, nothing special. An ordinary kind of figure. Plain dull. She's in his classes, thought Mashka. Lucky thing! Seeing Lyosha every day for three sessions in a row . . . She must be so happy! But then the girl in the glasses could easily be tormented by love for some unattainable fifth-year student. And not be happy at all.

Mashka wrote another note and addressed it to "Lyosha Sablin." She pinned it up on the board. At the next break the note was gone. That meant Sablin must have read it already.

But he took his time answering.

Mashka walked up to the board and glanced it over. Nothing . . .

During the next break Nastya came up to her.

"Has he answered?"

Mashka shook her head.

"Well, never mind," Nastya consoled her. "Maybe he's writing you a poem . . . Have you seen him?"

Mashka shook her head again.

"Well, never mind," Nastya repeated. "Maybe he's writing you a poem . . ."

They heard someone laughing. Sablin was standing in front of the bulletin board with the girl in glasses. His arm was around her shoulders and hers was around his waist. They stood there holding each other and laughing. Probably because they were happy. Because they were together. She said something to him in a loud voice. He didn't answer. But he smiled.

Mashka felt her cheeks freeze.

"Poser," Nastya snapped scornfully and Mashka clutched at the word as if it were a lifeline.

Of course he was a poser! And it was all just to make the unknown "M.N." realize that he was on a different planet from her. He didn't love that girl in glasses. He was just pretending . . .

"Don't get upset," said Nastya. "Maybe they're just friends."

"Sure!" said Mashka with a stupid smile, and then repeated it. "Sure!"

"Just don't go crazy. You're never going to get his attention anyway."

"Why not?"

"Because you're a naïve creature and he's a poser and womanizer. You don't need each other. If two people are going to be together, they've got to breathe the same air. But you'd choke to death in his atmosphere. And so would he in yours."

"I'm not bothered."

"He's good-looking, all right. He's even clever; I'll give you that. But you two are on different levels. He can't even see you."

"But I can see him!"

"Because you're craning your neck looking up from below. But he's way above you and he never checks the soles of his feet."

"So what can I do about it?" Mashka raised her eyebrows pleadingly.

"Nothing. Don't get too close to him. Just watch. And realize he's not God's gift to women," Nastya answered, spitting a husk into her hand.

Mashka started thinking. First, she and Sablin weren't schoolkids anymore. Second, he was a nice guy. Third—there was the girl in glasses. She'd known him for three years. She might even have gone to school with him. She had Sablin fenced off with little posts and velvet ropes, like in a museum. Look, but don't come close. You might get an electric shock.

"And anyway," Nastya went on, "you came here to study. If you fail this term's exams because of that good-looking creep, you'll regret it for the rest of your life."

The only words Mashka heard were "good-looking."

"Yes . . . that's what he is. Good-looking. Intelligent. Kind . . ."

"You don't know a thing about him!"

"I can see right through him . . ."

"So what do you see? Lungs, stomach, large intestine, small intestine . . . liver."

"And a heart! A big, passionate heart full of love!" Mashka closed her eyes dreamily.

"The heart is nothing but a hollow, cone-shaped muscular organ."

Nastya could belittle anything. Love was the desire to copulate. Purely physical. Sablin was a womanizer and a poser . . .

Mashka wrote another note. Pinned it up. The next morning the note was gone. And there was no answer. That night Mashka gnawed on her pillow, trying not to think about Sablin being out of reach, so that she wouldn't cry.

"Forget about him," Nastya advised her.

"I will," Mashka said compliantly.

When Nastya had gone, Mashka tore a sheet out of her notepad and wrote in big letters: "You're killing me. M.N. to L. Sablin." Now it was finished.

When Mashka came out of the lecture hall after class, by force of habit she went over to the board and started in surprise . . . A scrap of paper with the familiar letters "M.N." Written carelessly, a sprawling "m" with a long first stroke and the "n" just two lines of different length with a line through them.

It was her note. Obviously Sablin hadn't had a spare piece of paper. Or perhaps he simply didn't want to waste any on the unknown M.N.

"That's interesting. How is it possible to kill someone remotely? How are your studies going, M.N.? I wish you happiness and love, M.N.! Cheers!!! A.S." The words were written around Mashka's "You're killing me . . . M.N." For a few seconds she forgot how to breathe.

"Heavy. That's pretty heavy," said Nastya, cracking a sunflower seed.

"But what does he mean by 'remotely'?"

"At a distance, probably. What a literate bastard, eh?"

"Yes, he's classy!" said Mashka, biting her lips to keep herself from laughing, like that girl did with Sablin in front of the bulletin board.

"So you love him remotely," Nastya chuckled. "That's the way it is."

"He's so good!" Masha said, jubilant.

"He's polite," Nastya corrected her, spitting a husk into her hand. "You got on his nerves with those notes of yours. But he can't just send you to hell! That's not polite . . ."

"Listen," said Mashka, folding up the note, "do you want to live like that?"

"Like what?" Nastya didn't understand.

"Like you do. They're all posers and womanizers. But polite. They're all pretending. All trying to fool each other. Is that how you want to live?"

Nastya forgot to put the next seed between her teeth. Mashka turned around and walked away.

She sat down in the empty lecture hall and wrote a long letter that covered half a page in her notebook. And then she added a poem she'd written herself. If you read the first letters of the lines vertically, they spelled "LYOSHA SABLIN."

The note hung there for two days.

Nastya walked straight past Mashka, without acknowledg-

ing her, and Mashka didn't try to stop her. It was the week-
end soon . . .

The trees were on the brink of unfolding their leaves. They
were afloat in a tender green haze. Mashka went over to the
window and leaned her head against the glass. Who needed
her? Was there anyone who needed her? Nastya, who could
stick her between her teeth and crack her open? And then
spit out the husk. Did she need her? That polite poser and
womanizer Sablin? Who had the girl in glasses. Did he need
her? Outside the window snowflakes were swirling through
the air in the cold spring sunshine. Through the glass they
looked like poplar fluff, fuzzy and warm, that would settle
on her hand if she held it out. As if it were summer
outside . . .

The second class was Russian literature. Mashka was
hanging around in front of the bulletin board when she suddenly saw Sablin. Really close to her. He approached the
board, looked up at the notices and then spotted Mashka's
note. Pulled it down and opened it. Mashka watched his face
intently. Sablin smiled. And then again. He looked up.

"Did you like it?" Mashka blurted out.

"Did you write it?" asked Sablin.

"No."

"I really ought to read it on my own," said Sablin. "I can
feel myself blushing . . ."

Mashka nodded and went into the lecture hall. There
was no wind in her face. She was breathing freely and easily.
Her cheeks weren't freezing at the touch of the poplar fluff.
Nothing had happened. Sablin had glanced down under his

feet. So what? Nastya was sitting on a desk nearby, chewing sunflower seeds and spitting the husks into her hand.

There was no reply for two weeks. Mashka wrote all sorts of nonsense, everything she'd heard about him from other girls, and stuff like "Hi, Sablin. I'm doing just great. Write! M.N." Sablin took down the notes and he was obviously glad for M.N., thought her life was in good shape, that she didn't need any answers from him. Nastya chewed on her sunflower seeds and when she spotted another note addressed to "L. Sablin" on the bulletin board she laughed knowingly with a sideways glance at Mashka or Sablin—depending on which of them happened to be nearby.

"I told you so," she said, going up to Mashka after yet another failure.

Mashka sighed.

"Leave him alone. Forget it."

"I can't," Mashka almost groaned.

"Yes you can. I had to do the two-kilometer run for P.E. I spent half an hour telling the teacher that I'd never do it in less than twelve minutes, that I'd fail. So they said, get on with it then. If you prove you can't, no problem. So I ran it." Nastya put another seed in her mouth.

"And?"

"I did it without stopping in ten minutes twenty-eight."

"But that's just P.E. . . . ."

"What, you think you can make an effort with your muscles but not with your brain?"

"But I love him! Can't you understand that?" Mashka gaped at her.

"You've got a crush on him. That's different . . ."

"I don't know . . ."

Mashka kept finding herself in his glance. She looked

straight into his eyes when he walked by, and traced the dotted line running from his pupils. She promised herself strictly over and over again that she wouldn't look. But then Sablin would be there, walking toward her again, and she was greedily searching for the highlights in his brown eyes. No doubt every time he saw her Sablin struggled to remember whether or not he knew this strange girl, wondering whether he should say hello, since she was staring so hard.

He did say hello once. Mashka and Nastya were walking along the hallway and Mashka was telling a joke about how "Pushkin liked to throw stones." Sablin came walking toward them in his crumpled sweatshirt. Mashka's eyes locked onto him and she stopped speaking. She was drawn irresistibly to his eyes, and they were staring at each other again. It went on for about three seconds as Mashka and Nastya and Sablin walked along intersecting straight lines. And Sablin said:

"Hello . . ."

Mashka turned her eyes away as if she were pulling her hand back from a scalding-hot kettle. Then she caught her breath. That took four steps. She stopped and turned around: Sablin was bouncing away from her like a girl, and the layered curls on the back of his head said: "I don't see you!"

Nastya stopped too and spat a husk into her hand. She looked at Mashka, then at the white glow of Sablin's sweatshirt in the gloom of the corridor.

"Forget him," she advised Mashka.

Mashka didn't hear her and shrugged her shoulders mechanically.

"What good is that remote idiot to you?" Nastya suddenly exploded. "He's . . ." Nastya struggled to find the right word. "A philanderer! He's not worth it."

"He's great . . ."

Nastya filled her lungs with air, ready to prove the opposite, but then just waved her hand in despair, realizing that words couldn't help anymore. If only it had been possible she would have rammed Sablin's "hello" back down his throat with her own hands.

"You haven't got a hope!"

"So?"

"When it comes to that idiot, you're getting to be an idiot yourself!"

"Everyone who's in love goes a bit crazy," Mashka said with a shrug.

Nastya tossed two more seeds into her mouth and cracked them both with a loud crunch.

Mashka wanted to talk to Sablin. To exchange at least a couple of words. "Did you like that?" "Did you write it?" "No . . ." That was all they had. She wanted just to get him to notice her. Just to feel that three seconds of Sablin's life had been spent on her, that they belonged only to her. Two breaths in and one breath out. Four circuits of the blood around his arteries and veins. And his brain, occupied for a brief moment with Mashka's image. Mashka was gradually degenerating, turning into some primitive organism.

Sablin didn't even suspect that he had any influence over the strange girl in first year who always looked at him as though she'd lost a hundred rubles somewhere on his face. Or perhaps it was herself she'd lost. He just walked along the corridor with his bag on his shoulder, in his crumpled sweatshirt and sloppy jeans.

* * *

Mashka wandered around town feeling like the sunlight was blocking up her nose. It didn't warm anything, but it shone with a synthetic fury. Dust got into her eyes, mingling with bitter exhaust fumes. She felt uncomfortable because her top had worked its way out of her jeans and was hanging in a lump under her sweater. The lipstick had come off her mouth and was drying up. She sighed, a pointless existence. Sablin, with his jeans and curly hair, just flew along, breathing free and easy. And his T-shirt definitely didn't ride up under his sweater. Sablin again . . . He didn't write. He ignored her. Despised her. Spat on her from above. And for what? For nothing. He was just a poser, a womanizer, a remote idiot. He loved himself more than anything else on earth. He probably didn't even love the girl in glasses. He just made love to her . . . that is, had sex with her. What did that have to do with love? Mashka adjusted the bag on her shoulder and her hair fell across her face. She swept it back with her dusty hand. A pointless existence. Everything was pointless. She climbed onto a bus that pulled up.

Sablin spent days at a time in the basement of the university, editing his broadcasts for the Moscow Echo and Romantika radio stations. It was hot; he wiped his sweaty forehead with the hem of his shirt. The rectangular screen glimmered into life again, reflected in his brown-glazed eyes.

"Lyosh, it's time to go!"

"Just a moment . . ."

He ran up to the fourth floor to get the history exam questions from one of his classmates. He came across the usual scrap of paper pinned to the bulletin board and remembered he hadn't answered the last time or the time before that. His bag slipped off his shoulder and crashed onto the floor. Sablin swore and shoved the sheets of paper through the zipper and into his bag. The pages got crumpled, but so what . . . The scrap of paper with the words "L. Sablin, Group 302" on it got squeezed up against a balled-up handkerchief in his left pocket.

"Sablin!"

"Coming!"

The girl in glasses dashed out of the lecture hall.

"Leshik!"

Sablin mechanically pressed his lips against hers; his bag fell to the ground once again. The exam questions scattered into the air.

"Will I see you?"

He was collecting the pieces of paper.

"Will you call?"

"Perhaps. Yes. Probably."

"I'll be waiting! You promised." She thrust her fingers into his thick curls.

"Yes. I'm sorry . . ."

Sablin pulled the zipper of his bag closed. Brushed the girl's lips again with his own, dusty and cold.

The steps flew under his shoes as he ran out of the building and toward the bus stop. A bitter wind dried his eyes and he felt thirsty. He wanted to drop everything, just give up and stroll away with his hands stuck in his pockets. But that was today. Tomorrow everything could change. And after all, he was already twenty-five; it was about time he was earning a crust and a piece of sausage for himself, his mother, his father and his brother.

He got onto the bus as it pulled up to the stop, closing

his eyes for a second, and then took his handkerchief out of his pocket and wiped his face with it. A piece of paper stuck to his palm together with the handkerchief. He opened the squared page: "Hi there, my darling. Congratulations on the start (or the end already) of exam week. Good luck! Write! Write me something! M.N." Sablin tucked the note into his pocket. The bus smelled of wet vinyl seats and exhaust fumes. He closed his eyes. Then he reached into the pocket of his jacket and put a sunflower seed into his mouth.

Mashka flopped down onto the seat and set her bag on her knees. The bag fell off. She leaned down to pick it up and felt a sensation like electricity. Sablin looked at her with tired, empty eyes and spat a husk into his hand. Once, in her childhood, Mashka had been seduced by the crystal gleaming of the frost on the handle of an iron snow shovel and she'd licked it. Her tongue had frozen to it. Now Mashka was frozen solid again, only it was her eyes that were stuck to Sablin. He put a seed into his mouth, then reached into his pocket and brought out another handful of seeds. He held them out to Mashka. She took a seed and put it in her mouth. She cracked it. Spat out the husk into her hand. Took another one.

Sablin chewed his seeds, feeling sleepy. Four stops later he got out, after tipping the remaining seeds into Mashka's pocket. He just scooped them out of his own pocket and put them into Mashka's, holding it open with his finger.

Mashka carried on eating sunflower seeds in a daze, with the warm, wet husks gradually forcing the fingers of her fist wider apart. She took another seed and her fingers touched a hard corner. She took out the folded piece of squared paper. "Hi there, my darling. Congratulations on the start (or the

end already) of exam week. Good luck! Write! Write me
something! M.N."

Outside the window, the rain pitter-pattered against the pane
and the smell of wet windowsills filled the air. The gray walls
of the university loomed up outside. Mashka and Nastya
were sitting on a desk, eating sunflower seeds and spitting the
husks into their hands. Sablin was standing in front of the
bulletin board. Curly hair, crumpled sweatshirt, sloppy jeans.
He turned and walked into the lecture hall, handsome and
pleasant, with a smile on his face. Yesterday was far away
now, and he didn't feel like giving up on everything anymore. Mashka waited for his face, but at the sight of those
brown-glazed eyes everything got jumbled up inside her
head. She'd been going to say "Hi," but Sablin just walked
straight past her. He wasn't interested in anything she had to
say. They were miles apart, on different planets—the idiot,
the poser, the womanizer.

Iyokha
the rottweiler

After my stories
The sea capsized,
But someone invented dry land
And things got better
By themselves.

Zemfira

Iiudka stood on the windowsill on the thirteenth floor of her apartment block, readying herself for the jump. She was a bit drunk, a bit disheveled. Her hair flapped and fluttered in the December wind. Her fingers felt like ice. Liudka had definitely decided to jump. Because it was the start of the third millennium and she was stuck at home alone. No one had invited her to go anywhere, no one had come to see her. And her parents had gone to some friend's house and refused to take her with them. On the table sat an opened bottle of champagne and a plate of sandwiches. There were forty minutes left until the New Year. The whole country would hear the bells strike twelve. But Liudka would already be gone. Her body would be lying on the asphalt and her

183

blood would mingle with the snow and freeze in shapeless lumps.

Someone rang the doorbell. Liudka started and slipped on the ledge, but she managed to grab hold of the window frame. Her icy fingers cramped solid. The wind caressed her bare legs as it flung the snow about.

Silence.

The doorbell trilled again. Liudka felt her fingers gradually going numb. Her life didn't flash in front of her eyes in a rapid sequence of color slides, the way it's supposed to at the moment of death. Instead she caught a clear glimpse of a shaved head and a pair of brazen eyes. *Lyokha the Rottweiler,* she thought as she unclenched her fingers.

She didn't even know him.

When her friend Seryoga, a financial manager, had invited her and Tanka to the bank's New Year party, Tanka got terribly irritable about it.

"Shit . . ." she said, flinging a silver dress onto the bed. "I don't really even want to go!"

"Why not?" Liudka asked in surprise as she spooned cherry yogurt into her mouth.

"Why not?" Tanka's eyes opened wide and went as round as two big blue buttons. "You know what hotshots they all are in that place? It's a bank, fuck it, they all think they're as big and bad . . ."

" . . . as a buffalo's balls," Liudka added.

"Exactly!" Tanka agreed, pulling off her sweater and squirming into the silver scrap of material. "Listen, I think this is a really stupid dress . . ."

The dress barely covered Tanka's backside and her legs stuck out from underneath it like two sticks. The sequins jutted out on her pointed breasts.

"It's for striptease, Galya told you."

"Shit . . ." Tanka began climbing out of it again, wriggling like a worm.

"Wear the cocktail dress," Liudka advised her.

"Why, are we going to drink cocktails at this place?" Tanka asked venomously, flinging the striptease dress into the wardrobe.

They didn't get cocktails to drink, but wine and champagne, followed by vodka and mineral water. Waiters opened the bottles and placed the corks in their pockets. Bank employees sat there, picking decorously at their salads and steaks. Bellies and breasts in tight-fitting expensive shirts and dresses, spangles in hair—all very low-key, no more than just a hint at their Superior Status. Tanka sat there fuming in her stupid cocktail dress—right down to her toes—and watched the financial managers dance a wild jig with the security men out on the dance floor. But when she saw that no one cared about her dress, she wriggled her way out into the middle of the rampaging crowd and started skipping up and down to the beat of the songs: *"New Year's dashing on its way, gonna happen any day!"* And Liudka, who was just as drunk, if not more, ate a banana and ran an unsteady eye over the security men. They were all choice specimens—tall and bulging all over with muscles.

"Who's that one?" she asked, nudging Seryoga with her elbow and pointing to a big bull of a man in a white shirt, dripping with roguish gangster charm, with a smooth-shaved head and brazen, frightening eyes.

"Aha . . . That's Lyokha," Seryoga replied gleefully. "The

driver. He lives quite near you actually. I've seen him out walking his Rottweiler on your vacant lot a couple of times . . ."

Lyokha's white teeth, sharp as a rabbit's, gleamed in the
ultraviolet light as he shook his powerful shoulders about.

"Tanka! Tanka!" Liudka staggered as she pushed her way
through to her friend, who was already clamped firmly in the
embrace of some programmer. "Come here!"

"Mm . . . what?" Tanka muttered, coming to her senses.
She pushed away the programmer, who wasn't offended in
the least, and followed obediently after an excited Liudka.

Skipping along, Liudka led her over to where Lyokha
was dancing, then pulled Tanka's ear toward her and informed her in a loud whisper:

"That's Lyokha the Rottweiler! Classy, eh?"

Swinging her hips, Tanka circled Lyokha in the crowd as
if she was dancing and when she got back she announced:

"Yeah . . . Pretty nice."

Liudka was still at school, getting poor grades in the
tenth class. So she hadn't seen much of life yet. She had
spent all her years in the same social group, and as far as she
was concerned the boys in her class were just individuals who
happened to have pimples, but no distinctive sexuality. They
had greasy hair, damp fuzz on the upper lips and smart-
assed delusions.

But Lyokha was the real thing. He was a man. As big
and brazen as a well-fed tomcat. And five years older than
Liudka. But the worlds of Secondary School No. 3 and a
bunch of criminals couldn't be further apart. People from
these two different atmospheres couldn't understand each
other. Maybe they could sleep together, but they could never
understand each other . . . Her interest in him was infantile;
his disinterest showed in the boredom in his eyes.

Liudka sighed. She didn't dare introduce herself to Lyokha, even though she was drunk. Tanka looked around and yelled above the music.

"These old guys have drunk a shitload and they're skipping around like goats! What a riot! They're just like normal people!"

"Are they supposed to gesture with their fingers stuck out like that, though?" Liudka yelled back.

"We-ell, they do work in a bank."

People were jumping around on the dance floor, getting wrapped up in everything—the loud music, the cigarette smoke, the drunken, beefy security guards, the mandarins on the table, each other. The air was so thick with goodwill it made your head spin more than the Flagman vodka.

Liudka danced with Seryoga, intoxicated by the atmosphere of happiness and hilarity, as light as helium. She drank in the smoke-filled air as if it were pure bottled water, putting the corks in her pocket . . .

It was almost morning when they went home, barely able to stay awake on the back seat of Seryoga's Opel. Tanka went to bed just as she was, in her cocktail dress, and crumpled it so badly it looked like a cow had been chewing it. In the morning they sat in the kitchen at Liudka's place, drinking coffee.

"Shit," said Tanka, sniffing. "What happened? I didn't come on to anyone, did I?"

"Nah . . . It's a pity, though. You could have found yourself a real bad hunk . . ."

"With balls bigger than a buffalo's, right?" Tanka chuckled. Then she propped her cheek on her fist pensively and thought out loud. "Hotshots are just idiots—all talk. But those were great guys. Normal guys."

"And what's the difference between one type and the other?"

"Hotshots," explained Tanka, "are the kind who yell: 'I'm going to rip your face off!'"

"And the big, bad guys?"

"They just rip it off."

Liudka was so terrified she stopped breathing and her teeth clamped tight shut. For a second she hung frozen in the icy air between the earth and the sky, as if she were suspended in formalin; then she plummeted downward.

Suddenly her arm was wrenched violently. With a crunch, like bones being chopped in the meat section at the market. There wasn't time for Liudka to make any sense of it. Was it her soul leaving her body? Through her arm? She felt a searing, scraping pain across her chest and stomach, then a sharp stinging as if someone were ripping off her frozen tights and taking off her skin as well.

The lock on the door was twisted slightly open with the metal bent away beside the tongue. A big black dog with whitish spots was sitting on the rug by the door with its tongue lolling out, snuffling loudly. And standing right in front of Liudka was Lyokha the Rottweiler, breathing as heavily as the dog and staring at her with intense, dark eyes.

"Stupid fool," he said with an angry sob.

"Who are you?" Liudka asked with dry lips, bewildered, looking for wings behind Lyokha's back.

Lyokha didn't answer; he walked around the room in a circle and sat down on the sofa, taking a swig of champagne from the mouth of the bottle. His hands were trembling.

"Who are you?" Liudka struggled to focus her eyes on his shaved head, trying to figure out if he was God Himself or just an angel.

Lyokha didn't answer. Instead he took another swig and shook his head.

"I was just out walking the stupid dog . . . then this fool, up in the window . . ."

Liudka gradually recovered her wits and the first thought that came into her head just slipped out:

"Was that you then, ringing the doorbell?"

"Who else? Pushkin, maybe? Fuck . . . You're lucky the door was only closed on one lock . . ."

Neither of them said anything for quite a long time. Liudka came to her senses and began inspecting her scraped, bloody legs and swollen arm.

"Where are the bandages?" Lyokha the Rottweiler snapped with a frown.

Liudka waved her hand vaguely in the direction of the kitchen and watched in silence as Lyokha rummaged through the drawers, swearing under his breath. She sat there stupidly, watching his strong, deft, roughed-up hands as they bound up her wrist and elbow. Then her legs. The dog lay on the mat and snuffled, rolling his bright, gleaming eyes.

"Tomorrow you'll go to the emergency room," he said with another frown.

He closed the window tightly, forcing bolts that were never used deep into their sockets. He even pulled the curtains closed. Then he pressed on the chrome-plated metal of the lock with his finger and forced it back into shape. Liudka stood up on trembling legs and sat on the edge of the divan, feeling that cold void below her over and over again. She shuddered, clutching at the softness of the sofa, cautiously testing the floor to see if it would collapse . . .

"Very nice to meet you," said Lyokha, putting his Rottweiler on its leash. "See you."

"Goodbye," Liudka murmured, gazing at him with unseeing eyes.

Lyokha slammed the door and left. Ten minutes later Liudka heard the cheery "Bo-ong . . . bo-ong . . ." on the television. She sat there huddled into the cushions and watched the fireworks display, hundreds of different-colored stars bursting in the sky. The screen lit up her pale face, a nervous flush just beginning to spread across it. The mat by the door was crumpled and out of place and there were small dirty puddles of half-melted snow gleaming beside it.

The dog's made a mess of the floor, Liudka thought mechanically. I ought to clean it up.

my beautiful ann

The damp walls of St. Petersburg loomed, heavy and massive. Fat angels winced as they gazed upward. Rain had been dripping sullenly from the heavens for weeks. The sky was shrouded in dirty clouds.

Rabbit was sitting on a bench, wrapped up in his raincoat. He was drunk. He'd never been drunk before. His hair was clumped together in a pigtail behind his head and drops of water were running down the back of his neck. Rabbit was crying.

Rabbit's girlfriend had dumped him. Yesterday. She told him, "Rabbit, you're absolutely fucking useless." Like a door slammed into his face. They were at a friend's place and the rain was falling outside with the same regular rhythm. Just like now. Only then he'd still felt happy, not like now. Yesterday was Genka Titov's birthday, and he'd danced with Rabbit's girl. Then afterward they'd kissed in the kitchen. But Rabbit was in another room, watching television and drinking fruit juice. Everyone was teasing him because he wasn't drinking vodka. Then he went into the kitchen and saw everything. And then he got drunk. For the first time in his life. Stupid fool.

His girlfriend had come out of the kitchen and asked him why didn't he realize it was a joke. Rabbit asked if this was a joke, then what was the real thing like. His girlfriend said he shouldn't be so stupid. And then she told Rabbit to get lost.

Rabbit had left the birthday party at one in the morning and set out to walk to the city center. He'd stumbled over some kind of metal rod and fallen into a puddle. And then fallen asleep. He'd woken up at five in the morning and went back. And now he was sitting on a bench outside the entrance to his girlfriend's apartment complex. He thought he'd dreamt she told him to get lost. He was crying, hoping he was right.

They got to know each other when they were put in the same group on a trip to Hungary. And then it turned out they both went to the same school. Rabbit fell in love. For the first time in his life. They used to stroll around town and Rabbit would buy her lunch at McDonald's. And take her to the Hermitage. It wasn't really clear what for. But back then he didn't know how to behave around girls. This girl had taught him. She told him, "Rabbit, I'm going to make you cool." Rabbit didn't understand what that meant and he smiled in embarrassment. He had transparent ears that stuck out and long front teeth. When he smiled, his ears moved away from each other, he got two dimples in his cheeks and his teeth stuck out. Like a rabbit's. But the girl liked that. What she didn't like was Rabbit's personality. Rabbit was too timid, too naïve and too honest. With himself and with other people. The girl had been trying to give him a makeover, but there was only one thing Rabbit wanted: for her never to disappear and always stay with him. He thought about her all the time, so hard he couldn't talk about anything. But then nobody asked him about anything much anyway. A Rabbit's just a rabbit after all.

Every day Rabbit used to buy ice cream and take it to the doorway of the girl's apartment complex and when she came out he handed it to her. But she would get angry. "Why do you have to be such a romantic idiot?" she used to ask him, licking the ice cream. Rabbit shrugged, and that irritated the girl too. The way Rabbit dressed irritated her, and the way he laughed and sometimes spoke so loud that people could hear him miles away. It irritated her that when they got off a bus Rabbit took hold of her elbow. It felt uncomfortable. That he was so dull and no fun to be with. That he was always serious and didn't understand jokes. She used to tell Rabbit that was no good, but he would just smile and his transparent ears would turn pink.

Rabbit was faithful, though. Her best friend. Sometimes she asked him: "What if I'm unfaithful to you?" and he answered: "I'll leave you." And that really was what would have happened.

But Genka Titov was good fun. And two years older than Rabbit. He was fifteen.

Rabbit pulled his raincoat tighter around him and looked up. He knew he would never forgive his girl. That was why he was crying. He couldn't help himself. He was a romantic idiot and a man with principles. He couldn't just trample on his principles. It would be like deliberately jumping into a big heap of shit with a smile on his face. With those dimples.

The front door opened and Rabbit's girl appeared. She came over to him and Rabbit's face broke into a smile.

"Where's the ice cream, then?" she asked.

"Just a moment," said Rabbit, leaping to his feet. "Wait there!"

He ran to the shop, stumbling over his raincoat.

Genka Titov sat on his bed at home, strumming his guitar and singing: *"And I thought, does it really matter where you spent that night and who you were with, my beautiful Ann . . ."* His friends were lying asleep on the floor beside him.

postscript

mark wants to see me gurgle and choke in the Jacuzzi. I realized that this morning when I was standing in the shower blinking into the mirror. He was shaving, pulling his lips down into the shape of the letter O. He was probably waiting for me to slip so then he could stand on my hair. I'll suffocate and die. Then Mark will drag my pale pink body out of the Jacuzzi and carry it to the bed, which hasn't been made yet, by the way. He'll put me on the bed and fetch the little knife with the red handle from the kitchen. He'll gouge out my eye with the knife and come into the hole. Then he'll go to the kitchen, have a cup of coffee and come back. He'll gouge out my other eye. And come again. He'll go out on the balcony and have a smoke. Then he'll come back again.

He'll start gouging out my nostrils. But the holes in my nose
are too small and he can't get it in there. Then he'll curse
and stick his knife into my mouth. Push it in and out. Then
he'll come. He'll get up, get dressed and go to work. He'll
come back in the evening. Without even getting washed, he'll
start making love to my corpse. He'll try it from behind.
Then he'll bite off one of my toes. A little toe. He'll rest,
have a cup of coffee. He'll come back with a carton of cream
and stuff it in everywhere he can . . . He'll cut off my right
breast, put it on his head, pretend to be an alien. Then he'll
cut off the left one. He'll get all bloody and have to go wash
his hands. In the bathroom he'll see the mop and decide to
see what happens if he shoves the mop in. He'll splatter
blood over the whole bed, but he won't get anywhere. Then
Mark will cut open my belly and start sticking the mop in
there. He'll start feeling dog-tired. He'll have a cup of coffee.
Then he'll get out his sports bag. He'll rip my head off and
put it in the fridge as a keepsake. He'll stick all the rest in
various bags and put the torso in the sports bag. He'll take
them out into the country and throw them in a river. He'll
come back and wash my head under the tap, then take it to
bed with him.

I can't let it happen.

Mark's still shaving. I step out of the shower and go into
the kitchen. I take the little knife with the red handle and go
up to Mark from behind and take aim. The best thing would
be to slash his neck. That makes it a sure thing. Otherwise,
he'll have time to rip my head off ten times over before I can
stab through the muscles to the arteries.

"Martha," he says, "let's take a trip to the country
today."

In the sports bag, I think to myself.

"What for?"

"We could go for a walk."

Mark's getting washed, inspecting himself in the mirror. He's handsome. At least, that's what he thinks. And I make it a rule never to contradict him.

"Shall we go, then?"

I weigh my chances of sticking the knife into Mark's neck. He'll obviously be able to grab my hand in time. He'll rip my head off right there in the bathroom. And he'll wipe the blood on the towel.

"Mar-tha . . ."

"Yes?"

"Can you hear me?"

I'll have to wait until he turns his back to me. And then slash his throat. That's it.

But Mark doesn't turn away. He pulls my face toward him and kisses it. What if I do it now? No, it won't work . . . Damn!

At breakfast today I realized Mark wants to stab me with the butter knife. He was sitting there spreading butter on a piece of bread . . .

death in the chat room

There I am sitting at my PC when suddenly there's this knocking. I hear it quite distinctly: "Knock-knock!" So who is that at two o'clock in the morning? Odd . . . I sit there, trying to ignore it. Then the door opens quietly and someone comes in wearing a loose robe. Carrying a scythe.

"Who are you?" I say, taken aback a bit at first.

"Death," he answers in a low voice. Kind of shy.

"W-w-why are you here?"

He just stands there, shifting from one foot to the other. Twirling the scythe in his hands.

"No reason," he says. "I was just walking by, so I dropped in. What's wrong? You don't mind, do you?"

"No," I answer, brightening up a bit. "What makes you think that? Come on in. Want some tea?"

He shrugs one shoulder, a bit embarrassed. Kind of shy. But he sits down anyway, right on the edge of a chair. I go to get the tea. Have to boil the water, don't I? And put the sugar in. Can't do without sugar, after all . . .

I come back into the room and there's Death sitting at the PC, running his fingers over the keyboard. Slowly. He obviously doesn't use a PC too often.

"What's that you're doing?" I ask.

"Just chatting . . ." he says, pleased with himself.

So fine. Let him have his chat. No skin off my nose, is it? I'm not a tight-ass.

I sit down beside him and look at the screen. Death's chatting; his username is "Nasty." Writing all sorts of junk. Saying hello to everyone. Sticking in smiley faces. He's got the hang of it.

Then after that we had some tea. With honey cakes too, by the way. I'm not tight. I don't begrudge Death his little treat. Let him enjoy it. After we had our tea, he got ready to go.

"Got to be going," he said. "Things to do. You know how it is."

"Sure," I agree. "Got to see to business. Drop in again sometime."

"Will do!"

And he smiles. Must have taken a liking to me. I'm a pretty giving kind of person. People like me.

He left. And I went back into the chat room. They must be wondering where I've gone. I go in—and there's no one there. Well, there is. But I can see all the messages are really ancient. The last one says: "There you go, idiots, don't say I didn't warn you!" It's signed "Nasty." I've seen that alias somewhere before . . . Ah, to hell with it. I'll go check out the soaps.

you and me

The one who's right isn't the one who's right, but the one who's happy.

i hate my body. It's too much bother. Always causing a hassle. Dress it, hold it up straight, keep your hands by your sides, put makeup on your face . . . And I have to do it all, because it's my ID. Without it I'm nothing.

I want to touch you, but I can't—I'm not the right shape. You wouldn't like it. You're interested in other people. But I want to fly around your head and breathe in your ear. Then you'll wrinkle your face up in that funny way and think how good you feel with me. You'll love other people and kiss their lips, but I'll get tangled in your hair and just sit there absolutely still. Later you'll be left all alone and you'll realize something's missing. Then I'll untangle myself and blow on your eyes. You'll half close them. I love you like that. You'll realize that you feel good. That it's spring and the leaves are opening. That someone loves you. And you'll love someone too. Not me. You'll be consumed with passion, bite your lips because you're so jealous. I'll absorb all the blood and the tears. You'll feel good, but I'll feel bad. You'll decide you've found your other half and you'll get married. There'll be two sons and a daughter. I even know what their names are. I'll be in your hair, in your eyes and lips. One day you'll find yourself caught between This Side and That Side. And someone will start shooting. I don't remember who. Afterward you'll be lying in the hospital. Your wife will leave you. She doesn't want to be with an invalid. Nobody wants to be with an invalid. You'll bite your lips and only see your sons and your daughter in your dreams. Then one day you'll ask:

"Where are you?" Quietly, so no one can hear.

But I'm not there. You think being dead is better than being an invalid? You don't want to live like this. You want to die. I know that if you die you'll be with me, but I don't want it to be that way. I want to breathe in your ear every spring. But I'm not there. Do you think it was just something that happened? Do you think it's easy to die for someone?

I'm not there with you. And now your blood and tears come back to you. You can't carry on like this. But your little boy talks to you on the phone.

"Don't die," he'll say, hiding from his mother. Whispering.

Another ten years will go by. You'll realize everything wasn't in vain. When you learn to move your legs. When you stand up and walk. And later when you run. A girl from the third floor will fall in love with you. Your older son will leave school and go to your old college. The dean will remember your surname because you were more talented and cheerful than anyone else. Your son will be just the same. You'll be proud of that. You'll get married again. Your autumn will be lit by the sunny crimson glow of fallen leaves. You'll have a daughter. You'll be the happiest man in the whole world. You'll buy her a big dog. A real one. You'll take your daughter for walks in her stroller, buy her ice cream and take her to the nursery school. And after that to primary school. You'll show her forests and meadows, teach her to love caterpillars and cats. Then later you'll have a grandson. You'll look into his eyes and feel afraid. You'll avoid him and your older son will take offense. You'll try to justify yourself, shouting and gulping down tablets. People won't understand you. They'll blame you. Your blood pressure will rise.

You'll lie on a sofa with Validol under your tongue. You'll swallow the tears you cry because no one wants to understand you. You'll whisper:

"They killed you in his eyes."

You'll take the dog and go away to another town. You'll suffer badly from the separation with your daughter. You'll cry. Your grandson will grow and go to nursery school. Your son will write to you, pleading that you can't remain enemies forever. You mean too much to each other. You'll come for a visit. You'll see your daughter and never leave her again. And then your grandson. You'll force a smile and tremble inside. You'll feel afraid the same thing will happen again . . . You'll look into his eyes and see rain. I love rain. So do you. You'll start to love your grandson. You'll curse yourself for not coming back sooner. But you couldn't have come back sooner. There's a right time for everyone.

You'll introduce him to the dog and teach him to fight. You'll show him the sky and the stars. You'll buy him a drum and he'll wake you up with his furious drumming. You'll be the happiest of men with him. You'll live surrounded by love. Your younger daughter will graduate from college and get married. Your second son will have twins— two little girls. The dog will die. Your grandson will grow up. He'll stay out all night, and you'll worry and drink Valocordin. You'll shout at him, and he'll do drugs and sleep with girls. You'll try to hammer it into his head that he's still too young, and he'll get furious with you for interfering in his life. You'll get tired and overstrain your nerves. You'll go gray.

Your grandson will write songs and sing them to strangers. You'll want to understand him. You'll decide that you mustn't lose him because of your own ambitions. You'll go to the club where he plays with his band. You'll get worked up and breathe in too much cigarette smoke. You won't recognize him onstage. Then you will. Then you'll hear his songs. And you'll realize that he's singing about me.

You'll leave the club. You'll stagger through the dark, damp streets, laughing and crying. You'll bite your lip so it bleeds and fall to your knees. On broken bricks. But you won't care. You'll shout, but no one will hear you.

You'll come home in the morning, as your grandson will. You'll run into each other outside the door and you'll smile at him. And he'll smile too. Then he'll go to bed, but you'll sit in the kitchen and smoke. Your wife will come in wearing her nightgown and you'll tell her you love her. A few more years will go by. Your daughter will get married, your eldest son will have a little boy and your eldest daughter will have a little girl. The twins will grow and start grabbing at your nose. Your grandson will get hooked on heroin. He'll die. You'll look into his glassy eyes and see the same stars that you used to show him. At the funeral you won't cry. Your eldest son will have a heart attack.

They'll bury your grandson in the ground. You'll go home and on the way you'll hear the sound of spring. You'll wrinkle up your face. You'll feel good. You'll ask:

"Why is it all so cruel?"

Do you think it's easy to die for someone?

It is.

isupov

I'm studying in the journalism program. But I haven't got a clue what I'm going to do when I graduate. I don't enjoy running around with a Dictaphone in my hand, pestering people with questions like: "Do you think Yeltsin will be elected for a second term?" I hate trying to decipher interviews. I die when the assistant dean assigns us a feature story to write. I do enjoy going to college. But the only person I'd really like to write about is Isupov.

He's got long curly hair and crazy eyes. He screws them up when he says hello to me. The way he talks is like his hair—long, tangled and pointless.

We met on Freshers' Day, when he was strolling around onstage wearing lipstick and a dress. Then he took off the dress and everyone could see his stomach. Most people fall in love when they look into someone's eyes. But I fell in love with his stomach. It just blows me away.

God help me, but I can't remember what we talked about on that historic evening. I kept trying to think of something clever to say that wouldn't just echo what Isupov had said to me. All I can remember is the lipstick on his mouth and his shifty eyes.

Natashka said: "He's a buffoon."

"How do you mean?" I was puzzled.

"I mean he's a clown."

"Why?"

"Because."

Natashka doesn't like anyone much on principle. She finds all earthbound people boring. She only likes musicians, stars. And if Isupov had gone onstage with a guitar instead of in a dress, Natashka would have fallen in love with him forever. I'm not that demanding. I even like men in dresses. Even with painted mouths and shifty eyes.

Isupov's nineteen.

"That's no age," said Natashka. She only likes men over twenty-five. She thinks they're not posers and clowns. She reckons by twenty-five all the folly of youth drains out of the male organism, leaving the seriousness and reliability behind. Maybe by twenty-five Isupov will be serious and reliable. But in the meantime he's a clown. He's got long front teeth like a rabbit's. And his ears stick way out too. When he ties his hair back in a ponytail his head looks like a sugar bowl with two handles. That makes Natashka feel sick. She can't understand how anyone can live with ears like that. I reckon it all depends on how you look at things. From where I stand Isupov's teeth and ears look really good.

"You only look at him from one side," says Natashka. "But there are always two sides to every coin."

If Isupov's a coin, then I want him in my pocket. Apart from me, there are two other girls in our year who love Isupov and one who's given up on him. She even wrote poems about him for a newspaper. Only she changed the name.

"Why?" I asked her.

"So he won't get too cocky," she said spitefully.

I hope I never reach that stage. The other girls have set up their own debating society and they hold sessions in every class. The theme of the meetings is something like "What a great sweatshirt he's wearing today" or "That Isupov's a jerk and everyone knows it"—depending on what mood they're in.

I don't lower myself to childish stuff like that. When the tender feelings start oozing out through my ears, I look for the bunch of people that usually has Isupov in the middle and I listen to his jabbering.

"He's a waste of space," says Natashka. "He'd die without someone to entertain. He can't get anyone's attention any other way."

"I think he can."

"Yeah, right," says Natashka with a malicious laugh. "If he shows off his stomach. *Sasha's so sexy,*" she says in English. That's one thing I agree with her about.

"When there's no one to entertain, he starts running around the department pestering people he hardly even knows," says Natashka, deciding I want to hear her acute observations.

"He's just cheerful."

Natashka chortles like crazy and taps her forehead with her finger.

"Yeah right! Real cheerful!"

Yesterday something really important happened. Natashka got to know Isupov, or rather, he tried to hit on her. From their conversation it turned out he draws a total blank as far as I'm concerned. That amused Natashka so much that she got herself thrown out of Russian class. Out in the corridor she met Isupov again and spent ages trying to wind him up, but she was disappointed, because Isupov didn't understand any more than half of her jibes and caustic remarks.

I gave Natashka a call today. She was furious because I'd "dragged her out of the bathroom."

"Natash, will you do me a real favor? I'll love you forever," I said, crawling.

"This has got something to do with that ferret of yours, hasn't it?"

"Yeah . . . Introduce me to him, will you?"

There was this grunting at the other end of the line and then loud laughter. I waited patiently.

"Okay then!" said Natashka. "I'll set up take two!"

So the introduction's set for Friday. On Thursday I'm standing outside the Central Delicatessen selling sunflower seeds. My mom's disabled so she goes to Polyclinic No. 6 regularly, even though they never tell her anything new or anything definite. But anyway, once a month I get to stand outside the Central Delicatessen, shivering and ashamed in the cold damp air. I'm afraid someone from my class will see me and think I'm a bum or maybe the child of an unhappy home. But I have a happy family. My father died four years ago from one of his drinking bouts. Ever since then Mom and I have gotten along just fine.

There are sparrows circling my sack of seeds. The other saleswoman, fat red-faced Anya—known as "the Fat Fool"

behind her back—waves her arms at them, but I don't
bother. I reckon they can't eat all that much and anyway we
ought to help our little brothers.

Aunty Anya's face gradually turns purple and she shouts
in annoyance.

"These sparrows are all your fault!"

I don't even react, because I don't think you should let a
woman with an ugly red face get to you.

Meanwhile these two young guys come up to us. Aunty
Anya instantly concentrates and turns away from me. I stand
there looking down into a puddle because I don't like it when
pimply specimens ogle me out of the corner of their eyes. One
of the guys has a brown jacket. It looks familiar. I look up. He
looks, but he doesn't recognize me. Then just in case he says:

"Hello."

I nod, but I don't say anything.

"You're a fool," said Natashka later. "Why didn't you introduce yourself?"

"How?" I croak hoarsely, afraid I'm going to burst into
tears.

"You say: 'Sasha? I've seen you around! What's up, don't
remember me, jerk?'" Natashka's getting into her part now.
"He says 'No . . .' So then you say: 'Beat it then, you scabby
ferret!'"

"Just come straight out with all that?"

"Well . . . You could just clock him!" Natashka suggests.
"He'd remember that for the rest of his life!"

Natashka always has these radical urges.

The next day I saw Isupov in front of the mirror in the
entrance. With this intense look of concentration on his face
and his hairy hands. But basically looking pretty good. I went
up behind him and stood so close I could smell him.

Isupov turned around and screwed up his eyes.

"Hello," he said.

I nodded quickly.

"Hi."

He had a silver lion hanging on a cord around his neck.

"How're you doing?" I asked.

"Fine," answered Isupov. "And you?"

I could see from his eyes he was trying to remember who I am.

"I'm doing fine too."

"Yep . . ." said Isupov, and he looked straight past me over my shoulder, then up at the ceiling. I saw his small mouth with little black hairs sticking out all around it; obviously he's not too good at shaving. He really is a ferret, I thought.

Meanwhile Isupov was glancing around, probably wondering how he could get away from me as quickly as possible. He probably couldn't entertain one person at a time. He needed a crowd.

"Want some seeds?" I asked.

Isupov suddenly looked at me instead of through me. I wanted to stroke his curly hair. And just touch him.

"Um . . . I've got to go!" he said with a smile. "Bye!"

Natashka laughed for a long time over that.

about the author

Irina Denezhkina was born in 1981 and lives in Yekaterin-burg, where she studies journalism at the university. Since the publication in 2002 of *Give Me (Songs for Lovers)*, she has become a celebrated literary star in Russia and her book has become an international bestseller.

Printed in the United States
By Bookmasters